Rare Catholic Stories

Rose

A Treasured Collection

Rose is

RoseCalio

Little Way Press
Modesto, California
www.littlewaypress.com

The stories contained in this book were gleaned and adapted from Catholic readers published prior to 1892. A study guide for *Rare Catholic Stories* is available from Catholic Heritage Curricula at *www.chcweb.com*.

© 2007 Little Way Press
Cover art by Anne Simoneau
Cover design by RoseMary Johnson
Artwork on pages 116, 120, 158, and 161 by Kim Staggenborg

ISBN: 978-0-9764691-4-8

Little Way Press
Modesto, California
www.littlewaypress.com

Distributed by Catholic Heritage Curricula
P.O. Box 579090, Modesto, CA 95357
1-800-490-7713 *www.chcweb.com*

Printed by Sheridan Books, Inc.
Chelsea, Michigan
June 2013
Print code: 349080

Contents

One Good Turn Deserves Another

"Stop pushing, you little rascal," said a soldier who was standing near the edge of the sidewalk to watch the Corpus Christi procession.

"But I want to see," answered the boy to whom he spoke. "I can hear the music, but I cannot see a thing. The procession is coming out of the cathedral, and I shall miss the sight. I wish you would take me on your shoulders." The soldier did not answer. Indeed, before he had time to say a word, the boy had climbed up his back and was sitting on his shoulders. The crowd laughed, while the soldier good-naturedly allowed the boy to remain where he was.

The head of the procession was just in line with them. It was really a grand sight. First came the musicians, then the school children dressed in their best and wearing bright badges; next the college students and the different societies, carrying gay banners, then followed the clergy, and, under a canopy of white and gold silk, the Bishop bearing the Blessed Sacrament. Carrying the canopy were four of the leading men of the city, while after them marched a crowd of pious people.

"O, how beautiful, how beautiful!" cried the boy, while in his joy he hammered with his heels on the soldier's breast. "Ah! here come the altar boys. How I wish I were with them!" said he, and, the next mo-

ment, with a "Thank you, sir," he slid to the sidewalk, and was off toward the cathedral.

When the crowd dispersed, the soldier walked about the city, but afterward strolled back to the cathedral to see the procession returning. Imagine his astonishment, when among the altar boys, in red cassock and white surplice, he spied his young friend. As long as the procession remained in the cathedral, the boy was not noticed, but when he went to the sacristy to disrobe, the priest who was master of ceremonies at once detected the strange face.

"Who are you?" he asked, severely. "How do you happen to have that cassock on?"

"Please do not scold me, Father," replied the boy. "A kind soldier let me sit on his shoulders to see the procession, and when I saw a number of boys whom I know marching along, I could not keep from joining them. I know where the cassocks and surplices are kept, so I slid down, ran to the sacristy as fast as I could, and dressed myself. Then I cut across the city, came up with the procession, and here I am."

As he stood in the red cassock, his face bright with happiness, the sunlight, creeping through a stained glass window, shed round him a halo of gold. "Do not be angry with me, Father," he continued earnestly. "I was so happy, and it was all so beautiful!"

"So you would like to be an altar boy, eh?" asked the priest.

"O, indeed, indeed I would!"

"Then come with me," said the priest, and the two went out of the sacristy together.

* * * *

Fifteen years later, a French general lay wounded on a battlefield. The battle was not ended, and it was probable that the soldier would lie on the ground for some time; just then a chaplain passed.

"You are wounded, General," said the priest, as he bent over him.

"Yes; I am wounded in the leg. I can not put my foot on the ground."

The priest looked steadily at the wounded man,

as if trying to recall something, and then said: "Suppose I try to carry you on my shoulders, General. I can take you to the hospital wagon, which is not far off."

With some difficulty and much pain, the general got on the chaplain's back, who then set off on a brisk run. Now and then a ball whizzed past them. "That must be meant for me," the chaplain would say. "You have had yours," and he laughed as heartily as a boy.

As they neared the hospital wagon, shouts of victory were heard. Soldiers fled in every direction, and the French flag was seen waving in triumph. "Is it not a beautiful sight, General?" cried the priest, as he caught sight of the flying flag. "Almost as beautiful as the one I once saw from your shoulders."

"As you once saw from my shoulders?" said the general. "What do you mean?"

"Do you not remember the boy who perched on your shoulders one Corpus Christi? I am he. I knew your face as soon as I saw you, and thank God," he continued with a hearty clasp of the hand, "I am able to serve you now. One good turn deserves another."

What a Dollar Bought

"Good-bye, my son, and God bless you," said Father John, heartily, as he took his bag from Dick. "And here's a dollar for Christmas." With these words the good priest, who had been making his half-yearly visit to the little mission chapel in the mountains, sprang onto the train and was carried away into the gray, wintry twilight.

For a moment Dick stood staring, fairly struck dumb. A dollar! a whole dollar!—the first that Dick had called his own in all his fourteen years of life. True, he had earned honest wages, but they had come to him only in the shape of food and bed at the Hutchins' farmhouse, coarse homespun clothes, and an occasional pair of shoes.

Dick was an orphan, whom good Mother Hutchins had taken from the orphanage. Just before our story opens, the kind old woman dies; a daughter-in-law has come to rule in her stead, and now life is far from pleasant at the farm.

But there was always a roaring fire in the farmhouse kitchen, plenty on the farmhouse dinner table, and outside the wild, sweet freedom of the woods and the hills.

Twice a year Father John came, and Dick, by virtue of the good Sisters' training in the orphanage, became a very important person. It was he who scoured the woods for greens or flowers to deck the little altar, he who lighted the candles, served the Mass, and was sexton, sacristan, and master-of-ceremonies all combined.

"I hope Father John didn't mean this for—for—pay," said Dick, a sudden flush of honest pride dyeing his face as he looked at his dollar. "But he didn't—I know he didn't—he said it was for Christmas. But," continued Dick, shaking his head, "Father John shouldn't be throwing money around like this. There was a hole in his cassock and two patches on his boots—and—and—but I can't get it back to him now, so I'm going to do what he says: spend it for Christmas."

Christmas had never before presented any serious problems to Dick, but now matters were different. He stopped at the window of the village store where, amid an array of dolls, drums, and woolly dogs, lay three pairs of skates.

"My, but they are beauties!" murmured Dick.

"Hallo! is that you, Dick?" said a voice at his elbow, and Si Green's freckled face looked out from homemade cap and comforter. "Snapping weather, isn't it?"

"Fine," answered Dick, heartily.

"Maybe you think so. You wouldn't if you were I," answered Si, peevishly. "I can't go sledding or skating or anything, on account of this throat of mine."

"What, never again?" exclaimed Dick.

"Not this winter," was the hopeless answer. "Just when I had painted up that double runner of mine, and got her in prime order. I've a mind to sell her."

"What will you take?" asked Dick, his heart giving a sudden leap, for Si Green's double runner was the admiration of every boy on the Ridge.

"One dollar cash and not a cent less. It's worth more, but Jake Bond has an accordion that I'd like to have. It cost five dollars when it was new, but Jake says he will sell it for a dollar."

Dick fairly lost his breath. An accordion! Something to make music had been one of the dreams of his young life. He had sung, whistled, played the mouth-organ, but an accordion had been quite beyond his wildest hopes.

"Si," he faltered, "Si, would you feel very bad if I bought that accordion? I'd lend it to you whenever you wanted it; I'd come up here and play for you until you saw a chance of getting another. I've got a dollar—"

"You have!" said Si. "Where—where—did you get it?"

"It's a Christmas gift from Father John," was the proud reply.

"My! my!" gasped Si. "But I say, Dick, you can get an accordion almost any time. If I were you, I'd rather have Dave Whiting's pup. Prettiest thing you ever saw, real Newfoundland, all covered with soft, black, curly hair, and full of tricks already. Dave said he wouldn't take ten dollars for him, but his folks have sent for him to come to town on New Year's, and he wants cash."

Dick's mind took another turn. A dog! A black, curly, leaping, frisking, four-footed chum that could live in the stable yard and feast on bones! Poor, lonely, orphan Dick's heart gave a jump of delight at the very thought. "Where can I see him?" he asked.

"Down at Cissel's," answered Si. "Dave is staying there, and you'd better strike a bargain, if you can."

Dick started off for the Cissel farm, a Christmas thrill in his breast, as he thought of all the new delights that had suddenly come within his reach.

"Skates, sled, accordion, or pup! I can have any one of them. It's pretty hard to choose. But the pup!" Dick drew a long breath of delight. "A black, curly fellow, licking my hand and jumping at my call and running to my whistle, watching for me and loving me—that's the best of all. I'll just lay out that Christmas dollar in love, if it's only a dog's." Dick quickened his steps and wheeled briskly around the turn of the road that led past the little mission chapel, which was locked and deserted now after its three days of warmth and light.

As he stopped to look at the building, he caught sight of a figure apparently skulking near the arched doorway. "Hello!" he cried quite fiercely. "Come out of there. I am in charge of this church."

The figure came forward. It was an old, gray-haired man, shabby and forlorn.

"You're in charge you say, lad? Then let me in— let me in. It's a sore burden I'm bringing to the foot of God's altar. Let me in to the priest."

"The priest!" echoed Dick. "He isn't here."

"Not here," repeated the old man in a trembling voice. "Sure they told me at the Gap he was holdin' a station here."

"He was," answered Dick. "But he has gone."

"O dear, O dear!" moaned the old stranger; "I've walked twenty miles this day to find him—I that haven't been to confession this forty years—"

"Forty years—whew!" exclaimed Dick. "It's about time you were squaring things up—"

"It is, it is," continued the trembling speaker; "and bitter years they have been. I've come now to make my peace with Heaven. But the just God has turned His back on me—I must die as I've lived. It's too late."

"Oh, look here, none of that," said Dick. "It's never too late, you know. Father John was preaching about that last night. He is going to stop at Flynn's station about fifteen miles from here—until tomorrow morning, and if you get on the next train you can catch him there."

"The next train," repeated the old man. "How can a poor beggar like me get on the train? Didn't I tell you I walked every foot of the way here? There's nothin' for me to do but to go back as I came."

A sudden thought flashed into Dick's mind; for a moment there was a fierce struggle in his breast. Then his hand went down into his pocket and brought out his Christmas Dollar.

"Here, take this," he said. "It will pay your way to Flynn's and back—"

"God bless you—it will, it will," almost sobbed the old man. "It is God's own angel that is opening the way for me."

"Lean on me," said Dick, a little huskily; there was a big lump in his throat, for he knew that skates, sled, accordion, and puppy all were gone. "Lean on me and move lively, and you will catch the 8:30 train. Come on."

Months afterward, Dick, coming home from work

one day, saw a familiar figure on the porch.

"Father John!" he exclaimed delightedly.

"Yes," was the cheery answer. "You didn't expect me so soon, but I've come on business—to pay interest on that little investment you made last Christmas."

"Sir?" said Dick, staring into the speaker's face.

"The man you sent to me with your Christmas dollar died last week in God's peace, thanks to your charity, Dick—and he made you his heir. He had only a poor little shanty on a few acres of rock, and at first I thought your property was not worth claiming. But it seems the railroad has been trying to buy it for the last ten years, and the old man refused to sell. Now they offer you two thousand dollars for it. You can go to school now, Dick, and with God's help, become a fine young man."

And a fine man indeed Dick became. On Christmas Day his beautiful home is bright with love and cheer. His own merry boys and girls gather around the tree laden with toys and gifts, not only for them but also for every poor little orphan child within his reach. And his thoughts go back tenderly to that far-off past, and he tells another curly-haired little Dick, who nestles at his side, the story of his first Christmas dollar.

A Daughter to Be Proud of

When Mr. Lent visited New York last summer, he called at the office of his friend Mr. West. After a long talk about old friends and old times, they parted, but not until Mr. West had made his friend promise to dine with him the following day. "For," said he, "I want you to make the acquaintance of my wife and daughter."

"Have you only one child?" asked Mr. Lent.

"Only one," answered West, "but she is a darling."

Among the many sights of New York, Mr. Lent wanted to see the beautiful Central Park; so, on leaving his friend, he stepped into a horse car. In a short time, four girls, each about fifteen, entered the car; they were fashionably dressed, and each carried a lunch basket. Mr. Lent learned as they laughed and talked, that they, too, were on the way to the Park.

They had not ridden far when the car stopped to take on a girl of twelve and a sick boy of four. The new-comers were shabbily dressed, and as they seated themselves at the lower end of the car, they looked anything but happy.

"I suppose *they* are going to the Park," said one of the four girls, with a nod towards the poor children.

"I suppose so," answered one of her companions,

in a scornful tone, "but I would rather stay at home than go in such shabby clothes."

"Yes, indeed," said another. "I think there ought to be special cars for the lower classes."

This was not spoken in a loud voice, but Mr. Lent knew that the poor girl had heard the unkind words. He felt angry, and was about to tell the young "ladies" what he thought of them, when one exclaimed, "Why, there is Sara! I wonder where she is going?"

Mr. Lent turned to look; at the same moment the car stopped, and a modest young girl came in. The new-comer was warmly welcomed by the four, who made room for her beside them. "Where are you going, Sara?" asked one. — "What lovely flowers!" said another, as she bent over to smell them. "For what fortunate one are they intended?"

"I am going to Jane Hall's," said Sara in answer to both questions. "She is sick, and I thought these flowers might cheer her."

Just then Sara noticed the poor children. Crossing over, she gently laid one hand on the little boy's head, and asked, "What is the matter with this little fellow? He does not look well."

Sara's smile was

so pleasant, her manner so gentle, that the poor child felt she was a friend. "We do not know exactly," she said; "Danny has never been well. I am taking him now to the Park, to see if the fresh air will make him feel better."

"I am sure it will," said Sara. "It is lovely there; everything smells so sweet and pure. But you ought to have brought your lunch along, for the air will make you hungry."

A flush passed over the little girl's face. "Yes, we ought to have, but, you see, we had nothing to bring. Our brother Tom, who works, saved these cents so that we could ride to the Park and back. Maybe Danny will forget to be hungry, there will be so much to see."

There were tears in Sara's eyes as she listened; she inquired where the children lived and wrote the address in a little notebook.

After riding a short distance, Sara left the car, but where she had found two sad children, she left two happy ones. Half of her bouquet was in the little girl's hands, while Danny held a well-filled lunch basket, from which he helped himself now and then.

"She said we could eat it all," he whispered delightedly to his sister, "every bit of it. What made her so good to us?"

The little girl whispered in answer: "Because she has a good heart."

When the Park was reached, the four girls hurried out. Mr. Lent carried Danny out of the car and into the Park, and before leaving slipped some money into the girl's hand. "That is for a ride in a Park carriage," he said.

The following day he called at Mr. West's house. "This is my wife," said the host, introducing a pleasant-looking lady, "and this," as a young girl entered the room, "is my daughter."

"Ah!" exclaimed Mr. Lent, as he took the girl's hand, "this is the dear child whom I saw yesterday in the street car. She is, indeed, a darling. God bless her," and then he related to his friend what he had seen and heard.

Little Beginnings

Part I

"Mother, can we have a bazaar?" asked Winnie, dancing into the room, her face beaming with the enthusiasm of a new project.

"A bazaar!" echoed Mrs. Madden, pausing in her sewing, and looking up with surprise. "What put such a notion into your head?"

"Oh, all the girls have them!" answered her little daughter. "They give a sewing-bee, and make ever so many pretty things. Then they arrange them all on a table in somebody's parlor, and their friends come and buy."

"What do they do with the money?" inquired her mother, amused.

"Do with it!" replied the child. "It is only hard to decide what *not* to do with it. Sometimes they spend it for cakes and ice-cream, sometimes for candy. Jennie Hall and Minnie Leslie made ten dollars at a bazaar they had last winter. They gave quite a party one Saturday afternoon. All of their class went, and had a perfectly *splendid* time."

Mrs. Madden put down her work and laughed heartily.

"I don't see anything funny about it," continued Winnie, pouting a little.

"Indeed!" said the lady, and she could not help laughing again. "But if you want a party, dear, I think we could manage it without such an effort to secure the necessary funds."

"Oh, that is not it! It would be so interesting, getting ready for the bazaar. It would give us so much to talk about and to plan for. We'd be kept busy for weeks," explained the little pleader.

"And who are 'we'?" queried her mother.

"May Carroll, Nan Lawrence, and I. Nan says *her* mother won't mind, and Mrs. Carroll told us she would be willing if you were."

"I have not the slightest objection to the bazaar, if you give the proceeds to some worthy cause," explained Mrs. Madden, gently. "A great deal of good might be done with ten dollars. It would be a small fortune to a homeless person. Let each of you select a poor woman to work for. There is Mrs. O'Neil, whose husband met with an accident recently, and is in the hospital. She has four or five small children, and it is a hard struggle for her to find bread for them all. Your share of ten dollars would buy her a bag of flour, and some warm article of clothing for one of the little ones."

"But, mother," faltered Winnie, with tears in her bright eyes, "we are only little girls, you know. Do you think we could help the poor just as grown ladies do?"

"Why not? You can have your bazaar with all the pleasure it is supposed to give you, and, in addition, make it a source of happiness to others. If you go to work with the right spirit, you will succeed, I am sure."

"Yes, that will be the very nicest way to manage it," agreed Winnie, giving her mother a kiss. "I'll run and tell the others."

The plan was received with great favor. Mrs. Carroll knew a destitute sick person for May to assist, and Nan declared that she would find a *protégée* for herself.

The following day being Saturday, the three girls met at Winnie's house, to look over their bits of satin, lace, etc., and see how they could be put to use for the bazaar. Their mothers had made sundry contributions to their store, in the way of ribbons, remnants of velvet, and other trifles, so that the prospects were very encouraging. As May could sketch and paint simple flowers very prettily, she set to work at once. Winnie knew something of embroidery, and Nan placed at her disposal the contents of her work-basket.

"I shall keep all the odds and ends," said the latter. "They will do to make pin-balls, needle-books, and to dress dolls—of course we must have dolls for the little ones who come to the bazaar. Then I shall crochet slippers—I know a new stitch." Nan had a talent for making the most of everything.

It had been snowing all day, but the girls were too busy to notice the dreary weather. Winnie and May were busy designing, and Nan was collecting her scraps, when she heard a shuffling, fumbling noise at the street door.

"Some one is trying to ring the bell," she said. "Minnie Leslie promised me a piece of plush to make a photograph case. Perhaps she has brought it over. I'll go and see."

She flitted away, but the next moment they heard her exclaim: "Oh, girls!"

They rushed into the hall. There was Nan, still holding the door-knob and silent with amazement; while standing in the vestibule was the strangest little creature they had ever seen—a bent, wizened old woman, not nearly as tall as the girls. A quaint hooded cloak of black enveloped the figure from head to foot. She carried a stout stick, upon which she leaned heavily for support. From the shadow of the hood peered two piercing eyes, set in a wrinkled face that looked like a piece of parchment.

"Oh, it's a witch! a witch!" cried May, in a frightened whisper, starting back into the sitting-room.

"No," said Winnie, detaining her. "She has not a cross face. Perhaps it is a fairy. Has any one here a fairy godmother?" And she laughed, as if still half believing the old, nursery tradition.

Meantime Nan had regained her self-possession. "Come in," she said, cheerily, holding out her hand to assist the aged grandam.

"Yes," added Winnie, remembering her duties as hostess, and stepping forward; "come and get warm."

May held back till she noticed that the features were almost blue with cold, and the aged frame seemed benumbed.

The old woman huddled down on the floor beside the fireplace in an ecstasy of delight, bowing and swaying her misshapen body to warm herself. Her first words reassured the girls: "Glory be to God, but it's good to feel a bit o' heat in these poor bones!" she ejaculated in a rich brogue.

"This is no impostor," thought Winnie, running off to get her a cup of hot tea, and to tell Mrs. Madden of the unexpected guest. May placed a chair for her, while Nan looked compassionately at the forlorn creature.

"Heaven bless ye, miss!" she continued. "May ye live to be as old as meself, and niver know a day of throuble!"

"And how old are you, ma'am?" asked Nan, timidly.

"Come Easter, it's a hundred year I'll be," was the reply.

Mrs. Madden, who appeared at that moment with Winnie, smiled in good-natured incredulity, but the young folk listened gravely. If their strange acquaintance had said she was two hundred, they would have been quite ready to believe it.

Nurse was sent home with her, with instruction to provide for her comfort; and soon returned, bringing the information that she was undoubtedly deserving of aid. She lived in a queer little attic, and earned the "bit of food to keep body and soul together" by minding the neighbors' children when the mothers went out washing, and the like. But now that hard times had come, things went ill with her friends, and often they had nothing to share.

"Well," said Nan when she heard the report, "I've found my *protégée*. I'm going to work for the old woman!"

Part II

The time sped happily away, till at last came the afternoon set for the bazaar, and with it a troop of friends to Mrs. Madden's cosy parlor, to admire and purchase the pretty articles which the children had made. They found, tastefully arranged upon the mahogany corner stands and the center table, an excellent display of sachet-bags, pincushions, glove cases, etc. Nan's birthday had occurred about that time. At her special request, she received a gift of a box of dolls, which she dressed so attractively that they now delighted the younger visitors, and met with a ready sale. May happened to be presented with a basket of *bonbons*, only the day before, which, of course, she kept for the bazaar; and this had given Winnie the idea of making a quantity of molasses candy. Mrs. Lawrence sent some delicious chocolate cake and a good supply of cookies.

Mrs. Madden had a great secret from the children that morning. Cook chuckled and looked wise, but could not be coaxed into hinting at it. Just as the company began to arrive she and Nurse smuggled into a corner a large freezer of ice-cream. The girls soon discovered it, and were most demonstrative in their gratitude. Nan then took charge of the refreshment table, and was soon doing a thriving business. Winnie and May were kept equally busy selling the dainty knick-knacks. Besides their schoolmates, a number of ladies came to help the charity, and lavished their bounty royally, the girls thought.

When evening came, and their patrons had departed, the three sat down to count their gains.

"Do you think, dears, that you have made ten dollars?" asked Mrs. Madden roguishly, that having been the girls' goal.

"Guess how much we really have, mother?" said Winnie.

"Fifteen, perhaps twenty?"

"More," said Nan.

"Can it be twenty-five?"

"More still," said May. "It is thirty! Just think—thirty dollars!"

They all gave a gleeful cry of triumph. The fund was then divided into equal parts, to provide for the wants of the O'Neil family, May's poor consumptive, and the fairy godmother.

"If you want to know what a real treat ice-cream or even oranges can be," said May a few days later, "just take some to a sick person who has been starving to death because she had nothing to tempt her appetite but bread and tea. Mamma and I have made our invalid as comfortable as possible. We have bought her some warm clothes, and mother says that every day when Cook makes dessert, I may lay aside some, and take it to her."

Good Mrs. O'Neil was overjoyed at the relief of her most pressing necessities.

"Och, alanna, this is a great help," said she to Winnie. "It will tide me over the time ag'in me husband is able to work ontce more."

As for Nan's aged friend, she declared she had been made happy for the rest of her life.

But this was not the end of the work. The next winter the mothers interested themselves more actively in the bazaar, and seventy-five dollars were raised. Another season many influential ladies took it up. Thus it went on; every succeeding year a larger sum was realized, till the proceeds amounted to hundreds of dollars; and hundreds of the deserving poor received timely aid and encouragement from it. Mrs. Madden was ever the prime mover in the enterprise, but when congratulated upon its success, she always gave the credit to the three children who had originated the plan.

"It's the old story, you know," she used to add, brightly; "oaks from acorns—grand results from little beginnings."

Little Joseph's Letter

In France, and in some other countries, there are people who earn a living by writing letters for those who cannot write.

Among these letter-writers in Paris was one known as Sergeant Peter; he was an old soldier, and had the reputation of being "as rough as a bear."

One day, as Sergeant Peter was sitting at his desk, smoking his pipe, and waiting for customers, a boy entered. He was a little fellow, about six years of age, with thick, curly hair, and big blue eyes that seemed used to tears. His trousers were worn at the knees, and his jacket was patched.

Going up to Sergeant Peter, he said politely: "Please, sir, I wish to have a letter written."

"All right," said the old man, picking up his pen, "it will cost you one cent."

"Then I am sorry that I troubled you, for I have not a cent," and the child turned to leave.

"Here! come back, come back," cried Sergeant Peter. "Are you a soldier's boy?"

"No, I am my mother's boy, and she is all alone."

"O, I understand. Neither of you has any money, and you want to write for some so as to buy something to eat. Well, I shall be no poorer for the few lines and the sheet of paper. To whom do you wish to write?"

The boy turned red. It was not easy for him to say to a stranger just what he wanted, but he took courage, and answered, "I wish to write to the Blessed Virgin."

Sergeant Peter laid down his pen, and looked up to see whether the boy was joking. But the honest face of the child told how much he was in earnest.

"What is your name, my boy?" asked Sergeant Peter.

"Mother calls me her little Joseph."

"Well, little Joseph, what do you want to say to the Blessed Virgin?"

"I want to ask her to wake up my mother. She went to sleep yesterday, and I cannot rouse her."

Rare Catholic Stories

Sergeant Peter felt tears coming to his eyes. He was afraid to understand little Joseph. "Why did you speak of something to eat a moment ago?" he asked.

"Because we want something to eat. Before mother went to sleep, she gave me the last bit of bread in the house. For the last two days she would not eat any herself, she said she was not hungry."

"Ah! I see. How did you try to wake her?"

"As I always do; I kissed her."

"Did she breathe when you kissed her?"

The boy looked up and asked, "Do not people always breathe?"

Sergeant Peter turned away to hide the tears that were rolling down his cheeks.

"Was your mother warm when you kissed her?"

"No, she was cold! very cold! But it is always cold now in our room."

"Was your mother pale?"

"I do not know what that is, but she was beautiful, so beautiful! Her hands were crossed on her breast, and were very white. Her head was back on the pillow, and her eyes seemed looking into Heaven."

"O, how ungrateful I am!" said Sergeant Peter to himself. "I am in the best of health, with enough to eat and drink, and plenty of clothes to keep me warm, while this poor child's mother starves to death, and yet I envy the rich."

Sergeant Peter drew little Joseph toward him, and said gently: "Little man, your letter is written and delivered. Take me to your mother."

While he was getting ready, the old man continued to talk. "I had a mother," he said, "a long, long time ago. I can see her now as I saw her for the last time. 'Be honest, my son,' said she, 'and be good, and you will be happy.'"

"Well, I have been honest, and now I mean to be a good Christian. Where my dear old mother is, there I wish to go, and I shall take you with me, my little man."

Sergeant Peter saw that Joseph's mother was buried like a Christian. Then he took the little boy home with him and adopted him. Years after, when Joseph had grown to be a man, he became a great writer, and, what is better, he always wrote on the side of truth and right.

Sergeant Peter still lives. He is a happy old man and a pious Christian, and is very proud of his little Joseph. When he tells the story of little Joseph's letter, as he often does, he says, "I do not know who the postman is, but I know that those letters are delivered without fail."

That Red Silk Frock

You could not help but like little Annie Conwell; she was so gentle. Unfortunately, she was not always a good child, for she was fond of her own way; and if she set her heart upon having anything, she wanted it without delay—right then and there.

Annie's great friend was Lucy Caryl. Lucy lived upon the next block; and every day when out on an errand for her mother, Annie called for her, or Lucy ran down to play. Regularly Mrs. Conwell said: "Remember, Annie, I want you to come straight from errands, and not stop at the Caryls'. You may go and play with Lucy afterward, but you must come home first."

"Yes, 'um," was the quick answer Annie always made.

But, strange as it may seem, although Annie Conwell was considered clever, she seemed to have a wretched memory in regard to this rule, or else there were many good excuses for breaking the rule. When, as sometimes happened, she entered the house some two hours late, Mrs. Conwell reproachfully looked up from her sewing and asked: "What time is it, dear?"

And Annie, after a startled glance at the clock, either stammered, "O mother, I forgot!" or else rattled off an excuse.

"Very well!" was the frequent warning. "If you stay at Lucy Caryl's without permission, you must remain indoors on Saturday as a punishment for your disobedience."

Nevertheless, when the end of the week came, Annie usually managed to escape the threatened penalty. One special holiday, however, her mother surprised the little girl by saying, "Annie, I have told you over and over again that you must come directly home, and yet for several days you disobeyed me. I am going shopping now, and I forbid you to go out to play until I return."

Annie reddened and glanced at Mrs. Conwell's face. There was no use in "begging off," so she silently walked to the window.

"It makes me so mad!" grumbled Annie, as she watched her mother leave. There was no use in standing idly thinking about it though, so Annie began to wonder what she should do. As she stood looking out the window, Annie saw Lucy Caryl who, from the opposite sidewalk, was making frantic efforts to attract her attention.

"Come into my house and play with me," Lucy spelled with her fingers in sign language.

Annie opened the window. "I can't, Lucy!" she called. "Mother said I must stay in the house."

"Oh, do come—just for a little while!" teased naughty Lucy. "Your mother will never know. We'll watch the corner; when we see her coming, you can run around by the yard and slip in at the gate before she reaches the front door."

The temptation was strong. Annie pretended to herself that she did not understand the uneasy feeling in her heart, which told her she was doing wrong. She ran for her coat and hood—little girls wore good, warm hoods in those days—and in a few moments was running along the sidewalk with Lucy to the Caryls' spacious brownstone house.

"My Aunt Mollie sent me some lovely clothes for my doll," said Lucy. "The box is upstairs. Wait a minute while I run and get it."

When Lucy again joined her friend in their accustomed play corner, Lucy, with much satisfaction, displayed her present.

"Your Aunt Mollie must be so nice!" exclaimed Annie. "How lucky you are! Three more frocks for your doll! Clementina has not had any new clothes for a long time. I think that red silk dress is the prettiest, don't you?"

"I haven't quite decided," answered Lucy. "Christabel looks lovely in it; but I think the blue one is perhaps even more pretty."

They tried the various costumes upon Lucy's doll, admiring the effect of each in turn.

"Still, I like the red silk dress best," said Annie.

"It would just suit your doll, Clementina, wouldn't it?" suggested Lucy.

"Yes," sighed Annie, taking up the little frock, and imagining she saw her own doll attired in its gorgeousness. After regarding it enviously for a few moments, she said: "Say, Lucy, give it to me, won't you?"

"Why, the idea!" cried Lucy, aghast at the suggestion.

"I think you should," pouted Annie. "You hardly ever give me anything, although you are my dearest friend. I made you a present of Clementina's second best hat for Christabel, and only yesterday I gave you that ring you asked me for."

These unanswerable arguments were lost upon Lucy, however. She snatched away the tiny frock, and both little girls sulked a while.

"Lucy's real mean!" said Annie to herself. "She ought to give it to me—she knows she ought! Oh, dear, I want it awfully! She owes me something for what I've given her."

"I am going home," Annie announced aloud.

"Oh, no!" protested Lucy, aroused to the sense of her duties as hostess. "Let us put away the dolls and read."

She packed Christabel and her belongings away again, and went to get some books. Annie waited sullenly. Then, as her friend did not come back immediately, she began to fidget.

"Lucy need not have been in such a hurry to whisk her things into the box," she complained. "To look at the red dress won't spoil it, I suppose. I will have another look at it, anyhow!"

She raised the cover of the box and took out the dainty dress. Still Lucy did not return. A temptation came to Annie. Why not keep the pretty red silk frock? Lucy would not miss it at once; afterward she would think she had mislaid it. She would never suspect the truth. Annie breathed hard. If she had quickly put the showy bit of cloth back into the box and banished the greedy wish, all would have been well; but instead, she stood thinking and turning the little dress over and over in her hands. In the meantime a hospitable thought had occurred to Lucy. She remembered that there was a new supply of apples in the pantry, and she had gone to get one for Annie and one for herself. On her way through the dining room, she happened to look out of the window.

"Goodness gracious!" she exclaimed; for there was Mrs. Conwell coming home!

At Lucy's call of "Annie, here comes your mother!" Annie started, hesitated, glanced at the box, and—alas!—crammed the red silk frock into her pocket. Then she caught up her coat and hood, and rushed down the stairs. Lucy ran to open the yard gate for her and thrust the apple into her hand as she passed.

Flurried and short of breath, she reached home just as Mrs. Conwell opened the front door. She did not hasten as usual to greet her mother; instead, she hurried to her own little room, shut herself in, and sat down on the bed to recover from her confusion.

As her excitement gradually died away, she found that, instead of feeling the satisfaction she expected in having spent the afternoon as she pleased and escaping discovery, she was restless and unhappy. Upon her dresser lay the apple which Lucy had given her. It was ripe and rosy, but she felt that a bite of it would choke her. Above the head of the bed hung a picture of the Madonna with the Divine Child. Obeying a sudden impulse, she jumped up and turned it so that it faced the wall. Ah, Annie, what a coward a guilty conscience can make of the bravest among us!

Glancing cautiously around, as if the very walls had eyes and could reveal what they saw, she drew from her pocket the red silk frock. She sat and gazed at it as if in a dream. It was as pretty as ever, yet it no longer gave her pleasure. She did not dare to try it on Clementina; she wanted to hide it away in some corner where no one would ever find it. Tiny as it was, she felt that it could never be successfully concealed. Remorse would point it out wherever it was hidden. Annie began to realize what she had done. She had stolen! She, Annie Conwell, had taken what did not belong to her! How her cheeks burned! She wondered if it had been found out yet. What would Lucy say? Would she tell all her friends? Would they avoid her, and whisper together when she was around, saying, "Look out for Annie Conwell! She is not to be trusted."

She covered her face with her hands, and burst into tears. And all the while a low voice kept whispering in her heart with relentless persistency until human respect gave way to higher motives. She glanced up at the picture, turned it around again with a feeling of sorrow, and, humbled and contrite, sank on her knees in a little heap upon the floor.

A few moments afterward her mother's step sounded in the hall. When one finds a little girl's coat flung on a chair and stumbles over a hood on the stairs, it is clear that the owner has come home in a hurry.

Mrs. Conwell had, therefore, discovered Annie's disobedience. She threw open the door, intending to speak to her; but the sight of the child's flushed and tear-stained face checked the words upon her lips.

"What is the matter, Annie?" she asked sternly.

"O mother, please don't scold me! I'm unhappy enough already," faltered Annie, beginning to cry.

Then, since the burden of her miserable little

secret had become unendurable, she told the whole story. Mrs. Conwell looked pained and grave, but her manner was very gentle as she said: "Of course, the first thing for you to do is to return what you have unjustly taken."

Annie gave a little nervous shudder. "What! go and tell Lucy I stole her doll's red silk dress?" she exclaimed. "How could I ever!"

"I do not say it is necessary to do that," answered her mother. "But you are certainly obliged to give it back. I should advise you to take it back without delay, and have the struggle over."

Mrs. Conwell went away, leaving the little girl to reflect upon the matter. But the more Annie debated with herself, the more difficulty she had in coming to a decision. Finally she started up, exclaiming, "The longer I think about it, the harder it seems. I'll just do it right now."

She picked up the dress, darted down the stairs, hurriedly prepared to go out, and in a few moments was hastening down the block to the Caryls'. Lucy saw her coming, and met her at the door.

"Did you get a scolding? Was your mother upset?" she asked; for she saw immediately that Annie had been crying.

"Oh, no!—well, I suppose she was," hesitated Annie. "But she did not say much."

"How did she happen to let you come here again?" continued Lucy, leading the way to the living room.

Annie cast a quick glance at the table. The box which contained Christabel and her wardrobe was no longer there. It was useless, then, to hope for a chance to quietly slip the red dress into it again.

"I'm not going to stay," began Annie. Her cheeks grew red; and Annie, finding herself so uncomfortable, stammered out the truth. "I only came to bring back something. Don't be angry at what I'm going to tell you. I took that red silk dress home with me; but here it is, and I'm sorry, Lucy, indeed I am!"

After the first surprise, Lucy thought that it must have required a good deal of moral courage to openly bring back the little dress. For a few moments there was an awkward silence; then she managed to say, "Oh, that is all right! Of course, I would have been angry if you had not brought it back, because I would have missed it as soon as I opened the box. I was mean about it, anyway. I might have let you take it to try on Clementina. Here, I'll give it to you now, to make up for being stingy."

Annie shook her head, and refused to take the once-coveted gift from her companion's hand.

"Then I'll lend it to you for ever and ever," continued Lucy, impulsively.

"No, I don't want it now," answered Annie.

The sense of having done right made Annie's heart light and happy as she ran home. She was even happier on the next Saturday afternoon as she knelt in church after receiving the Sacrament of Penance. The experience had taught her that one must learn to see many pretty things without wishing to possess them; and also that small acts of disobedience and a habit of meddling may lead further than one at first intends.

Annie became an obedient daughter and a most self-sacrificing woman; but she never forgot "that red silk frock."

Faithful in Little Things

"There is no use talking about it any more. I have to ride Bay Billy round the pasture till he is tired, and then go down to the post-office. So I cannot go with you and the other boys, much as I would like to go."

"Pshaw, Neil! What is the use of working all the time? I think a boy ought to have a vacation once in a while."

"I can do what I like in the afternoon," answered Neil, "but my father thinks a boy ought to learn to do all sorts of work."

"Maybe," said Leonard, as he turned to leave. Then looking back he called out: "Did I tell you that my father is going to buy me a bicycle next week?"

"No," replied Neil. "You are in luck. I wish I could have one."

When Neil put the letters in his father's hands, on his return from the post-office, he saw among them a bicycle circular. "How I wish I could have a bicycle, father," he said.

"Well, my boy, I am willing you should have one," answered his father, "when you earn it."

Neil's face fell at this, for he saw little chance of being able to earn enough money to buy anything so costly. "Leonard's father has promised to buy one for him," he added.

His father looked up. "He has, eh? Well, let me know the size of it when he gets his, will you? Has Leonard any work to do for his father?"

"No; he keeps out of the way till his father leaves in the morning, and is always asleep when he returns at night."

"Keeps out of the way, does he?" said Dr. Fox. "Well, my boy, if, at any time, you should see something you think ought to be done, I hope I can rely upon you to do it, without being told."

"I think you can, Father," replied Neil.

"Very well," said the doctor. "By doing your duty in little things you may, in time, gain large rewards. At any rate, you have the satisfaction of knowing you have done what you ought to do." As the doctor was leaving the room, he added, "Do not forget to let me know when Leonard gets his bicycle."

The next day was the third of July, and Dr. Fox was to leave home to attend a meeting of doctors to be held in the city. He expected to return on the afternoon of the Fourth, and the day following he intended to drive Bay Billy to a horse fair.

The doctor left no tasks for Neil, so he and a party of boys arranged to go berry picking on the Fourth, and as they had plenty of firecrackers, they expected to have great fun.

The morning of the Fourth was lovely, and, after breakfast, Neil started out to meet his comrades. As he was going by the pasture, he stopped to speak to the horse, and as he did so, the beast held up a hoof from which the shoe was dangling.

"O, dear!" said Neil, "why did you show me that now? I can not help you, old fellow." The hired men

Rare Catholic Stories

had all gone off for a holiday, and there was no one but Neil to take the horse to the blacksmith, who was three miles away. The boy knew that it would take most of the day to have the horse shod, as there were always so many horses waiting, and that meant giving up his day's pleasure.

It was a hard trial, but while Neil was thinking about it Leonard came up. "Come along, Neil," he said, "the boys are waiting for you." That settled it. Neil remembered what his father had said about doing what he thought ought to be done, and his mind was made up. "I am not going," he answered. "I have to take the horse to be shod," and he walked away.

The hatchet needed grinding, so he went to the house for it, and then returning, mounted the horse, and rode slowly to the blacksmith's, taking care that Bay Billy should not get lame from fast driving.

When Neil reached the blacksmith's, it seemed as if every horse for miles around was waiting to be shod. But Neil was a bright boy, fond of seeing what was going on; he watched the men at work, listened to what was said about the different horses, and busied himself so that the time passed quickly.

It was after three o'clock when Neil was ready to return home. Bay Billy started off in fine style; he had covered two miles, when Neil saw a man lying on the ground near the railroad station.

Getting off his horse, Neil hurried to the man's help, but on reaching him found he was in a drunken sleep, and, much to the boy's surprise, that he was the switchman, Leonard's father. Then Neil remembered that someone in the blacksmith's shop had said it was to be hoped the switchman was all right today, as there were so many extra trains, he would need all his wits.

What was to be done? It was impossible to rouse the man; Neil could not tell whether or not the switch was right, and the train that carried his father and hundreds of others might be along at any moment. There was no time to lose if a wreck was to be prevented. Mounting Bay Billy, Neil rode with all haste to a little hill, which overlooked the track.

With the keen edge of his freshly sharpened hatchet, it was the work of a few minutes to cut a long branch from a tree, to which he attached his red and black tennis coat; then remounting the horse, he waited for the train.

Rare Catholic Stories

As it came in sight, Bay Billy reared and plunged, but his young master held him in check with one hand, while with the other he waved aloft the danger signal and shouted to the engineer. Then came a sharp whistle, Neil saw the trainmen tugging at the brakes, the speed grew less and less, and finally the train came to a stop.

In a few minutes, the brave boy was in his father's arms. Later on, when all danger was past, the passengers were forcing on Neil a gift of money, while his father looked on, not knowing what to do. "What can such a boy do with money?" he asked. "He has no wants."

"Do with it?" roared a wealthy farmer, who with his son, had been on the train. "Do with it? Let him buy peanuts with it, if there is nothing else he wants; but do not deprive us of the pleasure of showing we are grateful to one who has saved our lives. What is such a poor, mean thing as money compared to the lives of those we love?" So the doctor had to give in.

That night, when talking over the events of the day, Neil said "I suppose, father, I can use part of my present for a bicycle?"

"No, my boy," said the doctor. "I think you should put the money in a bank. As to the bicycle, I mean to buy one for you myself, because I think you have earned it. You lost your holiday, but you knew your duty and did it."

A Miser's Gold

Part I

"Never mind, mother! Don't fret. We'll get on all right. This little house is much more comfortable than the miserable flat we have been living in. Now that Crosswell & Wright have raised my wages, we shall be able to make both ends meet this winter— you'll see!"

"Yes, dear, I'm sure we shall," Mrs. Farrell forced herself to respond. But Bernard was in great spirits, and for his sake she assumed a cheerfulness which she was far from feeling, as she bade him good-bye and watched him hasten away to his work.

"God bless his brave heart!" she murmured. "He is a good boy and deserves to succeed. It worries me that he has such a burden upon his young shoulders. What a shabby house this is! Well, I must try to make it as bright and pleasant as possible. I wish the girls were older and able to earn a trifle; every penny helps nowadays. Mary, indeed, might find a place to run errands for a dressmaker; but I can not bear to think of her going around alone down town. Besides, she is so bright and smart that it seems a pity to interfere with her studies."

With a sigh the mother returned to her duties, prepared breakfast for the other children and hurried them off to school. There were three: Mary, just twelve years old; Lizzie, ten; and Jack, who had attained the mischief-loving age of seven. Bernard was eighteen, and the head of the family. He was also the principal bread-winner, and earned ten dollars a week, which was a fine beginning for one so young. Still, it was not a great deal for them all to rely on, and his mother endeavored to eke out their scanty livelihood by taking sewing.

Life had not always been such a struggle for the Farrells. Before the death of the husband and father they had been in good circumstances. Mr. Farrell held for years a responsible position as accountant in one of the largest mercantile establishments of the city. He had a fair salary, which enabled him to support his family comfortably. But alas! an attack of pneumonia carried him out of the world in three days. Thus, they found themselves suddenly plunged into poverty.

The widow moved with her children to the third floor of a cheap apartment house. But the following year the rent of the flat was found to be higher than they could afford. They sought other quarters, and settled at last, just as winter was approaching, in the humble little house where we have discovered them.

The young people took possession of the new dwelling in high glee. They did not see the threadbare carpets, how much the house needed painting and papering, how decidedly out of repair it was. Only too glad of their satisfaction, she refrained from comment, tried to make the best of everything, and succeeded in having a cosy home for them, despite all difficulties. Despite her days of discouragement, she aimed to train her children to look upon the bright side of life, and to trust in Providence.

"Bernard," said she one evening, "I have been thinking that if I could hire a sewing machine I might get piecework from the shops, and earn more than by looking to chance patronage. I have a mind to inquire about one."

The boy was silent. She began to doubt if he had heard, and was about to repeat the remark when he answered:

"No, mother, don't. There are too many women doing that kind of sewing at starvation prices. But I'll tell you what would be a fine thing if you really had the time for it, though I do not see how you could—it seems to me we keep you busy."

"What is your idea?" asked Mrs. Farrell, eagerly.

"Well, if we could manage to pay the rent of a type-writing machine, I could probably get you copying from the firm as well as from some of the other lawyers in the building. I was wondering the other day if I could do anything at it myself, and thus pick up an additional dollar or two in the week. Of course, you would accomplish more than I could, and it would be a hundred times better than stitch! stitch! How I hate the whir of the thing!" And Bernard, with his juggler gift of mimicry, proceeded to turn himself into a sewing-machine, jerking his feet up and down in imitation of the motion of the treadle, and making an odd noise in his throat.

Mrs. Farrell laughed, as she replied: "I do not know that there is much choice between this and the click of the type-writer. But your plan would not do, because I do not know how to work the type-writer.

"There would be no difficulty about that," argued Bernard. "You know how to play the piano, and the fingering is much easier. It will come naturally."

His mother laughed again and consented to his project. Bernard spoke to Mr. Crosswell on the sub-ject; that gentleman became interested, succeeded in obtaining a type-writer for Mrs. Farrell on easy terms, and promised to send her any extra copying he might have. The manipulation of the machine did not, indeed, come quite as naturally as Bernard pre-dicted, but after a few weeks of patient practice she mastered it sufficiently to produce a neat looking page. Bernard brought her all the work she could do; it was well paid for, and a more prosperous sea-son seemed to have dawned upon the little home.

Just at this time the children took scarlet fever at school. They had the disease lightly, but what anxiety the mother endured! Thank God, they got through it safely; but there was the doctor's bill to be settled, and funds were at a low ebb once more. To cap the climax, when the house had been thoroughly fumi-gated by the board of health, and Mrs. Farrell was prepared to take up her occupation again, an attack of rheumatism crippled her fingers and rendered them almost powerless. Then it was that, worn-out and disheartened, she broke down and cried:

"Oh! why does not God help us?"

"Indeed, mother, He will—He *does*," said Bernard tenderly. "You are all tired out, or you would not speak in that way. You must have a good rest. Keep the rooms warm, so that you will not take any more cold, and before long you will be able to rattle the type-writer at a greater speed than ever. That reminds me, mother," he continued, "one of the things we have to be thankful for is that this house is easily heated. It beats all the way coal lasts here! The ton we got two months ago isn't gone yet."

"That is the way coal lasts when there is not any one to steal it, as there was in the flat," answered Mrs. Farrell, brightening up.

"No, there's nobody living immediately around here whom I'd suspect of being mean enough to steal coal," returned Bernard, carelessly, "except, perhaps, Stingy Willis. I don't think I'd wager that old codger wouldn't, though."

"I am afraid I should not have entire confidence in him, either," agreed Mrs. Farrell. But the intelligence that there was still coal in the bin had cheered her wonderfully. Repenting of her rash conclusion, she hastened to qualify it by adding, "That is, if half of what the neighbors say is true. But, then, we have no right to listen to gossip, or to judge people."

Stingy Willis was a small, old man, who lived next door to the Farrells,—in fact, under the same roof; for the structure consisted of two houses built together. Here he dwelt alone. He dressed shabbily, and was engaged in some mysterious business down town, to and from which he walked; not even a heavy rainstorm could make him spend five cents for a ride in a horse-car. And yet he was said to be very wealthy. Persons declared they knew "upon good authority" that he "had more money than he knew what to do with." Others delighted in fabulous stories concerning his riches. They said that though the floor of his sitting-room was carpetless, and the bay-window curtainless but for the cobwebs, he could cover the one with gold pieces and the other with bank-notes, if he pleased. Many were convinced he had a bag of treasure hidden up the chimney or buried in the cellar. Thus, according to the general verdict, he was a miser of the most pronounced type—"as stingy as could be," everybody agreed; and is not what everybody says usually accepted as the truth?

Certain it is that Stingy Willis acted upon the principle, "a penny saved is a penny gained", denied himself every luxury, and lived with extreme frugality, as the man who kept the meat-market and grocery at the corner frequently testified. Even in the coldest weather, a fire was never kindled in the house till evening; for over its dying embers the solitary man made his coffee the following morning. He had nothing to do with his neighbors, who really knew very little about him beyond what they could see of his daily life. They were almost all working people, blessed with steady employment. They were respectable, honest, and industrious; as Bernard said, not one of the dwellers in the street would ever be suspected of being "mean enough to steal coal," unless indeed Stingy Willis.

Part II

Gloomy days continued for the Farrells; they still had bread and oatmeal porridge, but that was all.

Who would have imagined their poverty! The little house was still distinguished from the others by an appearance of comfort. Although Mrs. Farrell could not do any typewriting, the children were neat and trim going to school; Bernard's clothes were as carefully brushed, his boots as shining, linen as fresh, his manner as gentlemanly as ever. The mother and Bernard had agreed to contract no bills; what they could not afford to pay for at the time they would do without. Mrs. Farrell still tried to hope for the best, but sometimes she grew dejected

It was unreasonable, to be sure, but sometimes Mrs. Farrell used to wonder how her neighbors could be so hard-hearted as to go past unconcern-edly. Often, too, as Stingy Willis went in and out of the door so close to her own, she thought: "How hard it is that this man should have riches hidden away, while I have scarcely enough to buy food for my children!" Then, reproaching herself for the rebellious feeling, she would murmur a prayer for strength and patience.

The partition between the two houses was thin. She and Bernard could frequently hear the old man moving about his dreary apartments, or going up or down the stairs leading to the cellar. "Old Willis is counting his money-bags again, I guess!" Bernard would say lightly, as the familiar shuffling to and fro caught his ear; while his mother, to banish the shadow of envious discontent, quietly said a decade

Rare Catholic Stories

of her Rosary.

The subject of the coal kept recurring to her mind with odd persistency. Repeatedly of late she had awakened in the night and heard the miser stumbling around; several times she was almost certain he was in her cellar, and—yes, surely, *at the coal*— stealing it piece by piece, probably. Then the noise would cease, and she would conclude she must have been mistaken. At last, however, it would seem that her suspicions were confirmed.

On this occasion it was after midnight, yet Mrs. Farrell was still occupied in a hopeless effort to patch Jack's only pair of trousers. The work was tedious and progressed slowly, for her fingers were stiff and the effort of sewing painful. Finally it was finished. With a sigh of relief she rested a moment in her chair. Just then the silence was broken by a peculiar sound, like the cautious shifting of a board. That it proceeded from the cellar was beyond question. A singular rattling followed. She rose, went into the hall and listened. Yes, there was no delusion about it: somebody was at the coal—that coal which, she remembered bitterly, was now but a small heap in the bin. That the culprit was Stingy Willis there could be little doubt.

Bernard had fallen asleep on the sofa an hour or more before. His mother called him in a low voice.

"Shh!" she whispered, signalling to him not to speak.

Once more came the noise, now more distinct and definable. The heartless intruder had become daring; the click of a shovel was discernible; he was evidently helping himself liberally.

Bernard looked at his mother in surprise.

"Stingy Willis?" he interrogated.

She nodded.

"And at the coal!" he exclaimed, suddenly realizing the situation, and now wide awake.

He crept down the stairs to the kitchen. Mrs. Farrell heard him open the cellar door with the least possible creak. She knew he was on the steps which led below, but he made no further sound. She had no other clue to his movements, and could only distinguish the rumble of the coal.

The suspense was ominous. What was the boy going to do? Why all this delay? Why did he not promptly confront the fellow and order him to be gone? In reality, only a few minutes had elapsed since she first heard the noise, but it seemed a quarter of an hour even since he left her. Should she go down herself, or call out to him? While she hesitated Bernard suddenly reappeared. She leaned over the banisters to question him; but, with a gesture imploring her to be silent, the astonished boy said, hardly above his breath: "Mother, come here!"

Cautiously she descended to the entry and through the kitchen to the cellar steps. All the time the shovelling continued. Whispering "Look!" Bernard blew out the candle he carried.

From the corner of the cellar in which the coal-bin was situated came the light of a lantern. Crouching down, Mrs. Farrell could see that it proceeded from a hole in the wall which separated the two houses. There was no one upon her premises, after all; but at the other side of the partition was Stingy Willis, sure enough! Through the opening she could just catch a glimpse of his grey head and thin, sharp features. Trembling with indignation, she peered forward to get a better view. Yes, there was Stingy Willis certainly; but—oh!—he was shovelling coal from his own into the Farrells' bin! As this fact dawned upon her she felt as if she would like to go through the floor for shame. Drawing back abruptly, she groped her way to the kitchen, and sank into a chair, quite overcome by emotion.

Stingy Willis alone had discovered their need. With a delicacy which shrank from an offer of aid which might offend, he had hit upon this means of helping them. Clearly, he had been thus supplying them with fuel for weeks—a little at a time, to avoid discovery.

"That, of all people, Stingy Willis should be the one to come to our assistance!" exclaimed the widow.

"And to think he is not Stingy Willis at all! That is the most wonderful part of it!" responded Bernard, enthusiastically. "He's a right jolly fellow!"

His mother smiled, appreciating his feelings as he went on:

"Yes, I'll never let anybody say a word against him in my hearing after this, and I'll declare I have proof positive that he's no miser."

"He is a noble-hearted man certainly," said Mrs. Farrell. "I wish we knew more about him. But, for one thing, Bernard, this experience has taught us to beware of rash judgments; to look for the jewels, not the flaws, in the character of our neighbor."

"Yes, indeed, mother," replied the youth, decidedly. "In future I'll try to see what is best in everyone."

The next morning Mrs. Farrell went about her work in a more hopeful mood. Bernard started for the office in better spirits than usual, humming snatches of a song, a few words of which kept running in his mind all day:

"God rules, and thou shalt have more sun
When clouds their perfect work have done."

That afternoon Mr. Crosswell, the head of the firm, who seemed suddenly to have become aware that something was wrong, said to him:

"My lad, how is it that your mother has not been doing the extra type-writing lately? I find a great deal of it has been given to some one else."

"She has been sick with rheumatism, sir," answered the boy; "and her fingers are so stiff that she cannot work the machine."

"Tut! tut!" cried the lawyer, half annoyed. "You should have told me this before. If she is ill, she must need many little luxuries" (he refrained from saying *necessaries*). "She must let me pay her in advance. Here are twenty-five dollars. Tell her not to hesitate to use the money, for she can make up for it in work later. I was, you know, a martyr to rheumatism last winter, but young Dr. Sullivan cured me. I'll send him round to see her; and, remember, there will be no expense to you about it."

"I don't know how to thank you, sir!" stammered Bernard, gratefully. Then he hurried home to tell his mother all that had happened, and to put into her hands the bank-notes, for which she could find such ready use.

Doctor Sullivan called to see Mrs. Farrell the following day.

"Why," said he, "this is a very simple case! You would not have been troubled so long but for want of the proper remedies."

He left her a prescription, which wrought such wonders that in a fortnight she was able to resume her occupation.

From this time also Mr. Crosswell gave Bernard many opportunities by which he earned a small sum in addition to his weekly salary, and soon the Farrells were in comfortable circumstances again.

By degrees they became better acquainted with old Willis, until he was an intimate friend of the family. Bernard had discovered long before that their neighbor, far from being a hoarder of wealth, was almost a poor man. He possessed a life-interest in the house in which he dwelt, and the income of a small investment gifted to him. In spite of his age, he still worked for a livelihood, distributing the annuity in charity. The noble-hearted old man stinted himself that he might be generous to the sick, the suffering, the needy; for the "miser's gold" was only a treasure of golden deeds.

Coals of Fire

George Benton lived in the country. Not far from his father's home was a large pond. His cousin Herbert had given him a beautiful boat, finely rigged with masts and sails, all ready to go to sea on the pond.

George had formed a sailing company among his schoolmates. They had elected him captain. The boat was snugly stowed away in a little cave near the pond. At three o'clock on Saturday afternoon, the boys were to meet and launch the boat.

On the morning of this day, George rose bright and early. It was a lovely morning. He was in fine spirits. He chuckled with delight when he thought of the afternoon. "Glorious!" said he to himself as he finished dressing.

"Now I've just time to run down to the pond before breakfast, and see that the boat is all right. Then I'll hurry home and learn my lessons for Monday, so as to be ready for afternoon; for the captain must be up to time."

Away he went, scampering toward the cave where the boat had been ready for the launch. As he drew near, he saw signs of mischief, and felt uneasy. The big stone before the cave had been rolled away.

The moment he looked within, he burst into a loud cry. There was the beautiful boat, which his

cousin had given him, with its masts and sails all broken, and a large hole bored in the bottom.

He stood for a moment, motionless with grief and surprise; then, with his face all red with anger, he exclaimed, "I know who did it—*unkind boy*. It was Frank Brown; he was angry because I did not ask him to the launch; but I'll pay him for this, see if I don't."

Then he pushed back the ruined boat into the cave, and hurrying on some way down the road, he fastened a string across the foot-path, a few inches from the ground, and hid himself in the bushes.

Presently a step was heard, and George eagerly peeped out. He expected to see Frank coming along, but instead of that it was his cousin Herbert. He was the last person George cared to see just then, so he unfastened the string, and lay quiet, hoping that he would not see him.

But Herbert's quick eye soon caught sight of him, and George had to tell him all that had happened, and wound up by saying, "But never mind; I mean to make him smart for it."

"Well, what do you mean to do, George?" asked Herbert.

"Why, you see, Frank carries a basket of eggs to market every morning, and I mean to trip him over this string and smash them all."

George knew that this was not a right feeling, and he expected to get a sharp lecture from his cousin. But to his surprise, he only said, in a quiet way, "Well, I think Frank does deserve some punishment; but this string is an old trick. I can tell you something better than that."

"What?" cried George eagerly.

"How would you like to put a few coals of fire on his head?" asked Herbert.

"What! burn him?" asked George doubtfully. His cousin nodded his head. With a queer smile George clapped his hands.

"Bravo!" said he, "that's just the thing, cousin Herbert. You see his hair is so thick he would not get burned much before he would have time to shake them off; but I should just like to see him jump once. Now, tell me how to do it—quick!"

"'If thine enemy be hungry give him to eat; if he thirst give him drink. For doing this thou shalt heap coals of fire on his head. Be not overcome by evil, but overcome evil by good.' There," said Herbert, "that is God's way of doing it, and I think that is the best kind of punishment for Frank."

You should have seen how long George's face grew while Herbert was speaking. "Now I do say, cousin Herbert," added he, "that is a real take in. Why, it is just no punishment at all."

"Try it once," said Herbert. "Treat Frank kindly, and I am certain that he will feel so ashamed and unhappy, that kicking or beating him would be fun in comparison."

George was not really a bad boy, but he was now in a very ill temper, and he said, sullenly, "But you have told me a story, cousin Herbert. You said this kind of coals would burn, and it won't at all."

"You are mistaken about that," said Herbert. "I have known such coals to burn up malice, envy, ill-feeling, and a great deal of rubbish, and then leave some cold hearts feeling as warm and pleasant as possible."

George drew a long sigh. "Well, tell me a good coal to put on Frank's head, and I will see about it, you may be sure of that."

"You know, cousin George," said Herbert, "that Frank is very poor, and can seldom buy himself a book, although he is very fond of reading, but you have quite a library. Now suppose—but no, I won't suppose anything about it. Just think over the matter, and find your own coal. Be sure to kindle it with love, for no other fire burns like that."

Then Herbert sprang over the fence and went whistling away.

Before George had time to collect his thoughts he saw Frank coming down the lane carrying a basket of eggs in one hand and a pail of milk in the other. For a moment the thought crossed his mind, "What a grand smash that would have been if Frank had fallen over the string!"

But he drove it away in an instant, and was glad enough that the string was put away in his pocket. Frank started, and looked very uneasy, when he first caught sight of George. But George at once asked, "Frank, have you much time to read now?"

"Sometimes," said Frank, "when I've driven the cows home, and done all my work, I have a little piece of daylight left; but the trouble is I've read every book I can get hold of."

"How would you like to borrow my new book of travels?"

Frank's eyes fairly danced. "Oh, may I? may I? I'd be so careful of it."

"Yes," answered George, "and perhaps I have some others you may like to read. And, Frank," he added a little shyly, "I would ask you to come and help to sail my new boat this afternoon, but someone has gone and broken the masts, and torn up the sails, and made a great hole in the bottom. Who do you suppose did it?"

Frank's head dropped on his breast; but after a moment, he looked up with great effort, and said, "O, George! I did it; but I can't begin to tell you how sorry I am. You didn't know that I was so mean when you promised to lend me the books, did you?"

"Well, I did wonder if you had done it," said George, slowly.

"And yet you didn't..." Frank could get no further. He felt as if he would choke. His face was as red as a live coal. He could stand it no longer, so off he walked without saying a word.

"That coal does burn," said George to himself. "I know Frank would rather I had smashed every egg in his basket than offered to lend him that book. But I feel fine." He took two or three somersaults, and went home with a light heart, and a grand appetite for breakfast.

When the captain and crew of the little vessel met at the appointed hour, they found Frank there before them, eagerly trying to repair the injuries. As soon as he saw George, he hurried to present him with a beautiful flag which he had bought for the boat with a part of his own money.

The boat was repaired and launched, and made a grand trip, and everything had turned out as cousin Herbert had said, for George's heart was so warm, and full of kind thoughts, that he was never more satisfied and happy in his life.

George found out afterward that the more he used of this curious kind of coal the larger supply he had on hand—kind thoughts, kind words, and kind actions. "I declare, cousin Herbert," said he, with a merry twinkle in his eye, "I think I shall have to set up a coal-yard."

Suzy's Dragon

Suzy sat in one of the great windows of the library, writing out her Latin exercises. It was dull work for her, for she yawned and fidgeted and sighed in a very restless manner. Every now and then she would stop in the middle of a line to watch the boys playing marbles on the sidewalk. There was little Kit and Jimmy Grant—what good times they had! Oh, dear! She wished she was playing marbles on the sidewalk, instead of toiling at these tiresome Latin exercises. Nobody had to study as hard as she did, she was sure. There was Tom, now, flying his kite! And there—yes, there was Ellen Hamlin going after trailing arbutus (a type of trailing strawberry plant that has pink and white flowers)! This was too great a temptation. Down went the exercises, and up went the window. She called, "Oh, Ellen! Ellen! Are you going after trailing arbutus?"

Yes, Ellen was going after trailing strawberries, and she wished Suzy would come with her. Why couldn't she? Suzy asked herself the same question, and she came to the conclusion that there was really no sufficient reason why she couldn't. "Because I can write the rest of my exercises out tomorrow morning," she thought.

"I'm just going for a walk to the Pinewoods," she said to Aunt Cathy, who had charge of Suzy and her brothers since their mother's death.

Aunt Cathy lifted her kind but penetrating gaze to Suzy's face, and Suzy felt uncomfortable, though all her aunt said in reply was, "Very well, my dear; you know best whether you can spare the time."

This was always Aunt Cathy's way. Suzy was the one who had lessons to learn—and Suzy was old enough to decide when these duties were over, and whether her lessons were learned. And if Suzy wasn't faithful to her duty, she would be the one to suffer.

Suzy always knew when Aunt Cathy thought she had neglected anything, and it always made her feel very uneasy. And now, over this lovely spring afternoon, searching for trailing arbutus with Ellen Hamlin, there was this shadow of uneasiness, of something unfulfilled, which clouded the bright day, and made the pleasure half a pain. But they were very successful in their hunt for flowers. Suzy had never carried home such a big basketful, and dear, kind Aunt Cathy admired them to her heart's content.

"But you look tired, Suzy," she said to her.

"Yes, we went farther than we meant to at the start; we went almost to Long Roads, Aunt Cathy."

"Which is almost three miles. I should think you'd be tired, Suzy. Now I should advise you, my dear, to eat your supper at once and go to bed."

And Suzy was sensible enough to take this advice, for she remembered what she had to do in the morning—and if she should oversleep!

"Will you call me when you get up, Aunt Cathy?" she asked when she went upstairs.

"You want to wake up at five o'clock?" exclaimed Aunt Cathy in astonishment.

"Yes, Aunt Cathy."

"Oh, well, I can do that easily; but it'll not be so easy for you to mind it," Aunt Cathy replied.

It didn't seem more than an hour to Suzy when she heard Aunt Cathy calling at her door, "Come, Suzy, it's five o'clock, and you remember you wanted me to call you."

"Yes, Aunt Cathy, I hear," she answered, "and I'm going to get right up," which she certainly meant to do. But it was so early, so long before seven o'clock, she would lie just a minute more. That was the last she remembered until a great thumping at her door broke into a morning dream.

It was her brother Tom. "Come, Suzy," he shouted, "aren't you ever going to get up? It's breakfast time. Come! Hurry up! I want you to see me fly my new kite. I bought it from Sam Green yesterday; it's the tallest kite you ever saw."

Suzy was horrified. Breakfast time! How could she have slept so long? Only an hour until her exercises must be ready! Was there ever such an unlucky girl? "Do go away, Tom," she said meanly to her brother, as she hurried into the library after a hasty breakfast. "I can't attend to your kite now, I'm in a hurry."

Tom flung out of the room in disgust. "I never saw such a girl in my life as you are, Suzy. You're always in a hurry, and you never get out of it."

She had no time to reply, for Tom had banged the door shut. Then what could she have replied? When the truth is told to us what is there for us to say?

But the fact was at present Suzy didn't think much about the saying; it was the doing that occupied her. Here were two pages yet to translate! She set to work now in good earnest, but of necessity, it had to be very hurried work; and Suzy was never a ready translator. She was always a little uncertain with those perplexing verbs and pronouns. She had no time this morning to go back and correct mistakes, however, for she was only at the foot of the first page when it was time to finish her chores before school.

Poor Suzy! It turned out to be a dreadful day for her. She got a bad mark, for that Latin lesson was an awful boggle, and another for not paying attention during math lesson.

"Dear me!" she sighed, almost in tears. "Everything has gone wrong this week. I suppose it's what Cousin Bella calls Fate."

"What does ail you, Suzy?" asked Aunt Cathy.

Suzy burst into tears. A dim consciousness was stealing over her that the "everything going wrong" wasn't Fate exactly.

Then Suzy told Aunt Cathy her troubles, how it all got worse and worse each day. Aunt Cathy listened gently and patiently, but at the end she did not say much. She felt sure that Suzy was finding out for herself the cause of these troubles, and she thought this would be better for her in the end than to have her fault held up before her by somebody else. Today, at least, Suzy was on her guard. She took her history lesson into a little back room, where she could neither see the boys playing at marbles, nor Tom flying his kite, nor Ellen Hamlin if she passed. Then she put her mind upon her task, and she was astonished to find that by this steady work, she had finished in an hour what she had many a time spent three hours over.

Suzy went into the parlor and found Aunt Cathy reading aloud to little Kit. It was a pleasant story. After the reading, which both Suzy and Tom had enjoyed as much as little Kit, they all began looking over the pictures in the book. Suzy came across a picture of St. George and the Dragon.

"Who was St. George, Aunt Cathy?" she asked.

"The legend of St. George is that he was a re-nowned prince, whose greatest achievement was the slaying of an enormous dragon and freeing a prin-cess from bondage. To everyone now it is a symbol of victory of some kind, the victory gained over any weakness or sin, for we all have some weakness or sin, which is a dragon for us to fight."

As Aunt Cathy concluded, Suzy's face grew very grave and earnest; and bending over the picture of St. George, she looked at it a long time in silence; but it was not until she was alone with Aunt Cathy that she spoke what was in her mind.

The boys had both gone to bed, and she still held the picture before her, regarding it with great inter-est, when she said, "Aunt Cathy, I've found my drag-on. It is that long word beginning with 'P,' that little Kit was trying to spell the other day. It means to keep putting everything off until another time that ought to be done right away."

"I know. 'Procrastination'—that is the word, Suzy."

"Yes, that is it; that is my dragon, and it's been the

cause of all my troubles, Aunt Cathy. Now I'll tell you what I'm going to do. I'm going to ask father if he will let me have this picture, and I'll hang it at the foot of my bed, and try to remember when I say my prayers that I've got a battle to fight every day, for I have, Aunt Cathy. Oh, you don't know what hard work it is for me to sit and study. If it isn't one thing, it is another that makes my mind wander. And then, at the end of an hour I don't know a word of my lesson. Somebody will call for me to go somewhere, and I think, 'Oh, well, I can finish the lesson tomorrow.' And then when tomorrow comes, all sorts of things will happen, so there won't be a bit of time. That's the way the dragon has gone on beating me, ever and ever so long and—I don't know, Aunt Cathy, but—but he always will." And here Suzy began to choke a little. The next moment she burst out bravely in a determined voice, "But I shall keep trying very hard to beat him, anyway."

"That's it, Suzy!" Aunt Cathy exclaimed. "Try 'very hard,' and with God's help, I know you will win the battle, my dear."

And Suzy was true to her word. She did try 'very hard,' and at last she won the battle.

The Prize Winner

A king once ordered a trial of good deeds among his people, and offered to give the winner whatever he might select as a prize. There had often been trials of strength, trials of speed, and trials of skill; but in the first, the strong oppressed the weak, in the second, the swift did not help the slow, and in the third, one tried to cheat the other. This, therefore, was the first trial with a really good object.

A day was set for this new trial, and the following morning the people were to meet at the palace, where, one by one, they were to be admitted to tell the king what good they had done.

When the time came, many were the queer stories told. One man said he had searched through the kingdom, but could not find any good deed to do.

"Hem!" said the king, "you might, at least, have mended your clothes. That would have been better than nothing."

Another allowed that he had seen many little things to do, but had hurried on all day in search of some great thing worthy of a prize.

"How foolish!" cried the king; "do you not know that you can reach the great only by way of the little?"

A third declared he had given in charity half of all he owned.

"And if I award you the prize, what would you choose?" asked the king.

"May it please your majesty," quickly answered the man, "I would like to have one of your palaces."

"Any one of which, as you well know, is worth a hundred times all you have given," said the king. "The prize is not yours."

And so it went on, till at last the king regretted he had offered a prize, for he began to understand that good deeds are often done only for the sake of a reward.

Last of all came a little girl; she had on a plain, clean, calico dress, her hair was neatly brushed, and her blue eyes had such an honest look, that the king felt sure she had done better than any of the others. But she had come only to look on, and when the king asked what good deeds she had done, the child answered, "May it please your majesty, I had no time yesterday to do good deeds."

"No time for good deeds!" said the king; "pray, what were you doing?"

"Mother was busy," replied the child, "so I fed the chickens, picked up chips, swept the kitchen, set the table, and played with baby to keep him still."

"Good," said the king, "but did you not want to try for the prize?"

"O, yes, indeed," answered the little one, "because there is something I want very much—but I had to give it up, for I was too busy. I do not know how to do good deeds, anyhow."

"I think you do," said the king, "and I intend to give you the prize. So now, my child, tell me what you would like."

The little one was surprised; she blushed and stammered, and it was only because she desired the prize so much that at last she answered in a voice hardly louder than a whisper, "May it please your majesty, I would like a little wagon for baby to ride in."

She received not only what she wished for but much more.

Potato

Part I

"Have you practised your music today, Nell?" asked Mrs. Layton, as Nell took up a story book which she hoped to read undisturbed until supper.

"No, Mamma; but I don't feel like it now," she replied. "This is a lovely story, and I want to finish it."

"I am sorry," said her mother gently, "but tomorrow your music teacher will be here. You had better go to the piano, and practice your lesson several times more."

Nell pouted, and threw aside her book impatiently.

"Oh, dear!" grumbled Nell to Lucy, who was making a dress for little Elsie's doll, "isn't this just perfectly horrid! Plaguey old music anyway! I wonder who invented the piano? He ought to have had more sense!"

Nell was fast talking herself into a dissatisfied mood. Lucy looked quietly up from her sewing, regarded her sister steadily for a moment, and said, reproachfully: "Nell—potato!"

The word had a magical effect. Nell stopped abruptly, then said in a pleasant tone:

"Why, thank you, Lucy; I forgot." And, cheerily humming a popular air, she went at once to her task.

Mrs. Layton, who had overheard the little conversation, paused in astonishment.

"What can be the meaning of this?" she wondered, laughing quietly to herself. "What new game have the children invented? I never knew before that there was so much virtue in a potato. It seems to be an excellent cure for pouting."

She looked toward the library, hesitant to ask for an explanation. From the parlor across the hall came the sound of a faithful running of scales—an evidence that Nell had set to work with a right good will.

"No, I won't spoil the joke, whatever it is," concluded the lady, upon second thought. "I'll await further developments."

The next Saturday, the children received a visit from Minnie Prescott. Now, Minnie was not a favorite with Lucy and Nell. Mr. Prescott was the owner of the largest mill in the city. Minnie's mother had died several years before, and the child had been flattered and spoiled. It was a bright March day, but Minnie did not like the idea of going out for a run in the clear, bracing air.

"Oh!" she cried, "the wind would blow the feathers out of my best hat, and the rough walks ruin my new patent-leather boots."

The girls tried to entertain her by showing their books and games.

"They are very nice, but my papa buys me prettier ones," she said. "Let's not look at them any more, but just sit and talk."

So Minnie chatted away, and the others listened while she rattled on, about the fashionable school to which she was driven every morning in an elegant carriage; about her pretty dresses; about the styles, past, present and to come.

At last the young guest pulled out a tiny jewelled watch, glanced at it, and cried affectedly, in apparent dismay: "Why, it's five o'clock! Papa must have sent the coachman for me."

Minnie wished her friends good-by, gave Mrs. Layton a dainty, bird-like kiss, and floated away, saying, "Thank you. I have had a perfectly splendid time. Come and see me soon, girls; and I will show you all my pretty things."

Nell and Lucy watched her get into the carriage; the liveried servant closed the door with a flourish, mounted the box, gave the word to the prancing horses, and with a spirited toss of the head they were off.

"There she goes!" said Nell.

"Yes, and I'm sure I'm glad," said Lucy, sharply; "She feels so important, and is so proud because she has a watch and a diamond ring. It's only a speck of a diamond, anyway."

"But it *is* one," replied Nell, who had been rather impressed by the general glitter and flutter about the visitor.

"Minnie is always talking about herself," Lucy went on. "She is just as disagreeable as she can be, with her airs and her showy clothes. I don't see why we can't have more nice dresses than we have. Two for school, and one for Sunday—that's the rule. Mamma says, even if we could afford it, we should not have more than that in a season, as she does not approve of little girls thinking too much of what they wear. She ought to have heard Minnie!"

Mrs. Layton, who was in the library writing a letter, was disturbed and noted with distress the thoughtless criticisms. "Lucy should know that my girls should be charitable in word and deed. Perhaps Minnie is irritating. But I cannot bear to see one of my children with a jealous or envious spirit."

Lucy was in the midst of another complaint; both were too engrossed to notice that Mrs. Layton had crossed the hall, and stood in the doorway. Just as she was about to speak, Nell laid her hand on her sister's arm and exclaimed, as if upon sudden thought: "Oh—oh—potato!"

To the good lady's amazement, Lucy cut herself short in the middle of a word. After a moment of silence she said, regretfully: "It was unkind of me to talk so about Minnie. She has no mother to tell her what to do, and is not so much to blame if she makes mistakes."

Mrs. Layton turned away. She was puzzled, to say the least. "What possible connection could there be between virtue and potatoes?"

She had not time to ponder the matter further, however, for a week before, a violent spring storm had burst upon that section of the country with relentless fury. When it had passed, it left rack and ruin in its track. The factories, of course, were closed. The "hands," so unexpectedly thrown out of employment, were left without the means of support. Some poor families had lost their all.

After initial efforts of prosperous neighbors to

assist the unfortunate families, the hapless victims of the flood were forgotten. Mr. and Mrs. Layton gave freely of their own means, and encouraged their friends to do so also.

Lucy and Nell worked well, too. They mended all the clothing that they had outgrown, that it might keep other children warm; and established a bank for all their odd pennies, which had formerly found their way to the corner candy store. This bank was to be opened when filled, and the contents spent for the relief of the needy.

The end was accomplished much sooner than the girls had dared to hope. When Minnie Prescott heard what they were trying to do, she became enthusiastic at once, for Minnie was a good-hearted child. Accordingly, the very next day the coachman drove to the door of the Layton house, bringing a bundle of the young lady's discarded finery, and a scrawl of a note in which was enclosed a five dollar gold piece, which had been a birthday present from her grandmother.

"How funny one of the poor McCartys will look in this!" said Nell, taking up a faded dress, elaborately trimmed with satin.

"But isn't Minnie generous!" exclaimed Lucy, turning the gold piece over in her hand. "She told me her grandma gave it to her to buy a lovely silver pin which she has been longing for."

Part II

"Hurry, Lucy! We'll be late for school," cried Nell one morning, a day or two after the above conversation. Lucy quickly collected her books and joined her sister.

They hastened to the pantry. Nell dragged out the potato basket and tipped out the contents; thereupon, both began picking over the potatoes, each anxious to secure the largest. Then occurred an animated discussion:

"You had the biggest yesterday; it's my turn now," said Lucy, disconsolately, as Nell held aloft a splendid specimen and started hurrying away. "It isn't fair!" continued Lucy; but a timely recollection flashed upon her, and she cried, in a remonstrating tone: "Potato! potato!

Instantly Nell stopped and came slowly back. She looked wistfully at her treasure, then unexpectedly dropped it into Lucy's lap, caught up another of goodly size, dusted it in a trice, and ran off.

Bridget, who was busy with her work, paused and held up her hands in wonder. "Wisha! what has come over the childer?" thought she.

Lucy meanwhile, looking a little ashamed, deposited the potato in her school-bag, and prepared to follow, leaving the rest scattered about the floor.

"Indeed, Miss," exclaimed Bridget, half in fun, half in earnest, as she surveyed the disorder. "I don't know how it is that ye young ladies can perform such miracles just by crying, 'Potato!' Troth an' it's 'Potato' I'd like to say to yerselves. Look at that dirt on me clane floor! An' whose goin' to tidy up the place, will ye tell me?"

"Oh, excuse me, Bridget!" replied Lucy. "I'll have everything in order in a minute." So saying, she returned, and began picking up the potatoes, and putting them into the basket.

"Och, sure niver mind, Miss!" protested the good-natured cook. "Don't mind, awinna. I'll see to that. It's late for school ye'll be, I'm afeard."

"No, there is really plenty of time," said Lucy, pleasantly; but, having finished her task, she tripped contentedly away.

Bridget watched her out of sight; then she dropped into a chair, and laughed heartily. Mrs. Layton, coming into the kitchen at that moment, looked inquiringly at her.

"Faith, mum," said she, rising to receive the orders for the day, "it's the quarest play that iver was played. You have only to say 'Potato!' to thim, and they become as gintle and obadient as young lambs. But I dunno what it manes at all at all."

"So you have noticed the odd doings too?" said her mistress, smiling.

Thus encouraged, Bridget narrated the episode which had so surprised her.

"Well, this *is* very remarkable," said Mrs. Layton, as impressed with the story as Bridget could possibly have desired.

That afternoon, she said to her little daughters, when they were all enjoying a cosy chat together: "By the way, won't you let me into your secret? Perhaps your homely motto may do as much for me, as it has done for you."

"Secret—motto?" asked Lucy, in bewilderment.

"Oh, I know!" exclaimed Nell. "Mamma means 'Potato!'" And she laughed joyously.

"Why, that is no secret," said Lucy. "And we never thought of it as a motto. We are just making a novena of potatoes—that's all."

"A novena of potatoes!" repeated Mrs. Layton, rather surprised.

"Yes," explained Nell, eagerly. "At school we are having a novena for the Feast of the Annunciation. There is a practice for each day. The first day it was cheerful obedience, the next charity, and so on; today it was consideration for others. Then, as we all wanted to do something for the poor people who had lost so much by the flood, Mother Superior said that every day, each one who had kept the practice might drop a potato into a barrel; and at the end of the week the barrel would be given to a poor family. Any child who failed, after being reminded once, could not put one in, and nobody was to put in more than one. So we girls call this a novena of potatoes."

"And is the barrel nearly full?" asked Mrs. Layton.

"I should say so!" answered Lucy, with satisfaction. "In that corner of the corridor there are *three* barrels heaped high with potatoes."

"But what about the motto?" asked Mrs. Layton.

"Lucy and I agreed to help each other to remember the practice," replied Nell. "If she sees that I am in danger of failing, she says 'Potato!' If I notice that she is forgetting, I cry, 'Potato!' and we both understand. The novena will be finished tomorrow. Then, as we have such a supply of potatoes, several poor families are each to receive a basket. The nuns will add some meat, with everything that goes to make up a wholesome dinner. Mother Superior said if our mothers wished to send anything, she would be glad to add it to our little offering."

"I shall be happy to give you some fruit for the sick people," said Mrs. Layton. "The nuns have chosen an admirable method of teaching their young charges that charity begins at home, especially in the correction of our own faults. Though the novena is nearly over, I hope you will not forget the lessons you have learned."

For the next week Mrs. Layton had a secret of her own. At last, one day when Lucy and Nell came home from school, each was delighted to find in her own room a pretty oil painting of a cluster of beautiful white and purple blossoms.

"Aren't they lovely?" cried Lucy, rapturously.

"How kind of Mamma to paint them for us!" said Nell, gratefully.

"But what flower is this?" asked Lucy, looking closely at her picture. "It must be something rare. I've never seen it before"

"Look, here is a tiny scroll in the corner," interrupted Nell.

"So there is! Let us spell out the word in the scroll," suggested Lucy.

With eager curiosity they bent over their paintings.

"Why!" exclaimed Lucy, after a moment, beginning to laugh, "it's 'Potato!'"

"Well, if that isn't the nicest kind of a practical joke!" declared Nell, amused by the discovery.

"And actually," continued Lucy, pursuing her investigations, "I believe Mamma has painted for each of us a handsome bunch of potato blossoms!"

At the revelation, the two girls broke into a peal of merriment. Mrs. Layton heard their gleeful, ringing voices, and, coming into the room, joined in the mirth.

"But it is not all a jest," said the good mother. "I designed and painted these special pictures so that the flowers might remind you to cultivate, in daily life, the humble virtues which you have begun planting through your 'novena of potatoes.'"

The sportive homily was not forgotten, and, years afterwards, Lucy and Nell would show their children and grandchildren the paintings of the pretty white and purple flowers, and tell the story of "Potato."

Taddeo the Cripple

Father Pedro was visiting one day and said, "The boy should have some tools, some small tools, not too heavy for his weak hands, but with which he can amuse himself as he sits here by the hour in his low chair."

The boy's eyes grew bright as he heard this.

"Yes, yes, Mother! let me have some small tools, and I will make something for our own little altar."

"You shall have them, child; your father will be glad to do anything to make you happy."

That very night, when Julius the stone-cutter came from his work on the great cathedral, in the old town of Sienna, his wife, Catharine, told him what Father Pedro had said.

Julius listened with tears in his eyes. "Yes, my poor Taddeo, you shall have any and all the tools that your weak hands can use."

"Indeed, Father, my hands are not so very weak. If my feet and legs were only as strong as my hands and arms, I could climb with you to the top of the scaffold in the new cathedral. But they will grow stronger."

"That may be," said Julius, "but the tools you shall have." The next evening, when he brought Taddeo a set of small tools for carving wood, and a supply of soft wood that could be easily worked, there was not a happier child in all Sienna.

Poor little Taddeo had never taken a step in his life; for his feeble limbs were unable to bear his weight, slight as it was. But from this time there was no sadness in the large dark eyes, no quivering of the pale lips, as he saw other boys at their sports.

His prayers, even, were said with more fervor, and a ray of joy lighted up his face and his whole life. With the early morning his tools were placed by his chair, and he was at work. His mother did not ask him what he was doing, for she saw that it was to be a surprise for her.

The Advent days had come and gone, Christmas too, and even the Epiphany, but still Taddeo kept his secret. At last came the morning of the 25th of

March. Taddeo was dressed and in his chair ready to be taken to the early Mass, for it was the Feast of the Annunciation, and he wanted to receive Holy Communion on that day.

Presently he called his parents, and laid in their hands the figure on which he had been so long at work.

Catharine carefully removed the wrapping that still concealed it, and they looked with delighted eyes upon a rare carving of the Blessed Virgin.

"O Julius!" exclaimed the happy mother, "a real statue, and by our own little Taddeo!" And she clasped her boy in her arms, while tears of joy ran over her own cheeks upon his.

Julius, too, embraced his son, kissed him tenderly, and said, "Indeed, my Taddeo, you have worked with something besides those poor tools of yours."

"Only with my prayers, Father," said the boy. "I longed to do something for the Blessed Virgin. And now it is time; bear me to Mass, please."

Julius felt as if his child were a mere feather in weight that morning, so buoyant were the hearts of both; and when he carried him to Communion, and saw the joy that lighted up his pale face as he received his Lord, a feeling of almost reverential awe was mingled with his affection.

His statue was finished, but the thin fingers of the cripple were not idle. His brain teemed with holy fancies, and his skillful hands were never weary of giving them shapes of beauty. The wood was laid aside for marble.

Months passed away, and one evening, when Julius came home from his work, he told his wife and son that "every workman would, unaided, carve one pillar of the cathedral as an offering to the church."

The next morning Taddeo said, "Father, will you not take me with you today to the cathedral? I want to see the pillars, and to see which one you have chosen." For Taddeo to express a wish was enough for Julius. The boy was carried in his father's strong arms, just as he had been all his life, and the workmen at the cathedral made a seat for him.

His father had chosen a pillar near the altar of the Blessed Virgin, the second one, in fact. The first one, of the most beautiful white marble, had been left for some great artist, for some workman who should excel all the others.

Taddeo sat below, looking at the tall columns, and at the stonecutters seated high up on the scaffoldings around them, and a wish, a strong wish, swelled in his young heart. The workmen, as they looked down on the boy, said to themselves, "He is nearer Heaven than earth!" so holy was his look. They pitied him, too, because he was a cripple.

When Julius came down as usual at the noon recess, he asked Taddeo if he was not tired, and if he did not wish to go home. "No," said Taddeo, "but, Father, will you take me up to the top of the pillar, next to Our Lady's altar, and give me my tools, for that is the pillar I must carve."

"You, my son!" exclaimed Julius. "Why, Taddeo, that has been left for some great sculptor to do. None of us would think of carving that pillar."

"Ask Father Pedro," said Taddeo, while a look of pain passed over his face. "Ask him now, Father; I am certain he will not refuse me."

Julius consented because he was unwilling to deny his son, though he anticipated only disappointment; but Father Pedro, coming into the church at the moment, rendered the task easier. Laying his hand on Taddeo's head (for the boy was a favorite with him), he said, "What is it, my son, that you want me to say yes to?"

"I want you to say," and Taddeo spoke very slowly and solemnly, "that I may cut the pillar, the white marble pillar that stands nearest to Our Blessed Lady's altar."

Father Pedro looked surprised at first, then the tears came to his eyes. Finally, after a few moments silence, he said, "I will tell you tomorrow, after my Mass." Then, turning to Julius, "Be sure to bring Taddeo; I will see him directly after, in the sacristy."

* * * *

The Mass was ended. Taddeo was taken to the sacristy, and Father Pedro, before laying off his vestments, said, "You shall carve the pillar, my son."

Taddeo could not kneel, but he bent his head toward the hand of the good priest for a blessing, and then kissed it while a tear dropped upon it from his cheek. Julius took him in his arms to the church, and up the high scaffolding, brought him his tools, and then went quietly to his own pillar, close by.

Every morning after this, Taddeo was carried to his pillar, and his head was bowed low in prayer before he made a stroke with his chisel. Every night Julius took him home to his mother, weary but happy.

Months rolled by. The workmen no longer sit high up among the arches, but are coming lower day by day, and Taddeo among them. Now he has reached the very base, and every one stops to look at the tall white shaft that stands next to Our Lady's altar; for it is one column of pure white lilies!

It seems to bud and bloom with this same "plant and flower of light," for throughout its lofty height, no two lilies can be found exactly alike. Each has its six, open or closed petals, its thread-like stamens and its six large anthers, yet each one is unlike any of the others. The base from which spring shaft and capital is one mass of leaves, and among them Taddeo is carving a name in large, fair letters, also made of lilies. Beside him stand Julius and good Father Pedro. As he lays down his chisel he turns to Father Pedro and bows his head for a blessing, then leans forward until he rests against the pillar. Julius waits for him, for he is accustomed to seeing Taddeo lose himself in a moment's prayer. Then he stoops down to take up the boy as usual, but Taddeo is dead! He died with his head resting on the name he had carved among the lilies, the name of MARY!

Better than Riches

Part I

"Cash! Cash! Come here!" cried an attendant at the stationery counter of one of New York's great shopping emporiums. At the summons a delicate-looking little girl came wearily up, and held out a small wicker basket for the goods and the money. "Be quick now: the lady's in a hurry."

The child started off with no attempt at haste. The same words were dinned into her ears a hundred times a day. She did not see why ladies should be in a hurry. These ladies seemed to have nothing to do but to wear pretty clothes and to shop, which meant principally the buying of more pretty clothes. If she hurried every time she was told to, surely her tired feet would give out before the end of the day.

"Cash is so poky!" complained the sales girl to her companion behind the counter.

"Cash! Hustle I say!" called the floor-manager as he passed.

Thus warned, the child scurried away, and reappeared after a very brief interval. As she rushed up with the parcel, an awkward accident occurred. The lady heedlessly stepped backward. Cash dodged; but, alas! before she could stop herself, she had dashed into a pyramid of stationery that stood upon the end of the counter, and sent the boxes scattering over the floor in dire confusion.

"Oh!—oh my!" exclaimed the salesgirl, distressed, as she contemplated the wreck of the architectural display.

The disturbance at once brought the floor-manager to the spot. "Stupid!" he muttered, taking poor Cash by the shoulder. "Why don't you look where you're going? If you can't mind where you're going, we have no use for you here!"

"Please do not blame the child," interrupted the lady who had unwittingly caused the trouble. "It was my fault: I carelessly got in her way. I am very sorry."

"Don't mention it, Mrs. M——. It is not of the slightest consequence," said the floor-manager, with a smile and a bow. (Mrs. M—— was a desirable customer, and he would have said the same thing if she had happened to tip the glass show-case over.)

Cash, who was busily picking up the boxes, made a little grimace to herself at his change of manner. The lady politely inclined her head, and the floor-manager left abruptly.

When he had disappeared, the little girl looked up and faltered gratefully, "Thank you, ma'am!"

Mrs. M—— glanced down upon a freckled face and a tangle of reddish curls. Perhaps because the grateful glance touched a chord in the heart of the stranger, upon the impulse of the moment the lady did a very graceful thing. Taking a single rose from the bunch she wore, she fastened it to the breast of the child's black apron, and was gone before the latter could recover from her astonishment.

It was only a little incident, but it changed the whole aspect of Cash's day. The beautiful flower glowed against the dark uniform, like a bit of joy entrusted to a cheerless life.

"How lovely!" exclaimed the salesgirl. "Aren't you lucky, Cash! Don't you want to trade with me? I'll give you a delicious orange for that rose."

Cash shook her head. As soon as she could, she stole away, to the room where the girls kept their cloaks and hats. Here, after a furtive look around to see that no one was by who might snatch it away, she unpinned the rose and slipped it into a small cardboard box, having first carefully wrapped the stem in a piece of well-moistened paper. Then she tucked the box into the pocket of her jacket, and ran downstairs to the store again.

For the next two or three hours it happened that Cash was kept running to and fro almost without pause; but she did not mind it now. The kindly word spoken in her behalf by the truly gracious lady, the simple gift of a flower, had given her new spirit. Her heart, like a little bird, kept singing a cheery song to itself.

"Why, Cash, you're getting quick! What woke you up?" said the salesgirl, when, well on in the afternoon, the child sat down by the counter for a few seconds. Then, without waiting for a reply, she continued: "Now, aren't you sorry you did not exchange with me? See, you've lost your rose!"

"Oh, 'taint losted," answered the girl. "I'm keeping it for Ellie."

"Oh, sure enough! Poor Ellie! How is she? Here, I have the orange still; take it to her, too."

The child's eyes sparkled with pleasure as the salesgirl put the golden ball into her hand.

"Ellie'll be awful pleased. I'll tell her you sent it, Julia," she said.

Cash had, of course, another name: it was Katy Connors. The Connors were known among their neighbors as a respectable, although very poor, hard-working family. The father was a day-laborer; the mother went out washing; Joe, a boy of fourteen, worked as a messenger; after him came Katy, who was employed in McNaughton's store; and then Ellie, the little invalid.

Poor Ellie was fast becoming helpless. How different it had been a few months before! What a sturdy, active child she was, when one morning she set out in gay spirits "to earn money for Mother!" Like Katy, she had obtained a position as cashgirl in McNaughton's. How proud she felt when Saturday came, and she knew she would have two dollars and a half to take home! Unfortunately, it was to be dearly gained.

Saturday afternoon the store was unusually crowded. Little Ellie and her companions dashed now here, now there, in response to the cry of "Cash! Cash!" In the midst of the hurry, the floor-manager gave Ellie a message to deliver to a clerk in the basement. The child made her way through the throng, and was on the point of darting down the stairs, when, alas! her foot caught, she tripped, gave a little scream, and fell down the entire flight. In an instant several employees rushed to pick her up; but, to their alarm, though she strove to be brave, when they attempted to move her she gave a low moan of anguish. A doctor was sent for at once, who discovered that she had severe injuries, having struck against the edge of the iron steps.

Where now was the proud home-coming? Ellie was taken to the hospital. Upon one of the cots in the accident ward lay the child, her small face wan with pain. In one feverish hand she held something tightly clasped—something for which she had asked before being carried from the store. When the doctor turned aside she beckoned to her mother, and, with a pathetic little smile, folded into the palm of the weeping woman a small yellow envelope—Ellie's first wages, and the last which she was likely ever to earn.

The firm of McNaughton & Co. investigated the accident, but there was no loose nail in the stairway, not the least obstruction. The proprietors were not to blame; it was simply the child's heedlessness, they said. In fact, the fault was with Ellie's shoes: the sole of one, being broken, caught on the top step and caused her fall.

And she was to have had a new pair that very evening. Mrs. Connors had quietly determined that her first earnings should be expended in this way. Poor Ellie! she would not need shoes now: the doctors feared she would never walk again.

Part II

Not growing better at the hospital, Ellie begged
to be taken home. Rather than live apart from those
she loved, she strove to be content to remain alone
day after day, propped up by an inverted chair upon
a wretched bed. Or, when she felt stronger, with the
aid of a pair of rude crutches, she would drag herself to the window to watch patiently for the return
of the dear bread-winners, whose toil she would so
willingly have shared.

There, in a little stuffy room, upon the top floor
of the old house, she spent the long, hot summer;
there she remained when autumn came; there the
approaching Christmas holidays were likely to find
her.

How was it, then, that Ellie was usually cheery
and blithe? Perhaps her mother's prayer each morning, as she bade her good-bye to go to work, had
most to do with it. "May Jesus and His Blessed
Mother watch over you, mavourneen," the good
woman would say, with a sigh at the necessity for
leaving her. Frequently, when the child could have
wept for loneliness, the words would keep echoing
in her heart, providing comfort.

Ellie was keenly interested in everything that
went on. She thought there was no one like Mother,
but it was Katy who represented the world to her—
the world of McNaughton's store, with its bright-
ness and beautiful wares, and its ever-changing
crowd of ladies intent upon the pleasures of shopping. Any scrap of news which our little cashgirl
brought home at the close of the day was eagerly

listened to by her sister, who found her enforced idleness so difficult.

Katy had a great deal to narrate at the close of the day upon which our story opened. Sitting upon the foot of Ellie's bed, she told how she upset the pyramid of stationery; and what trouble she would have been in, but for the kind lady who so promptly came to the rescue. To Ellie's quick imagination the story had all the charm of a fairy tale. And when, at the close, her sister placed in her hands the orange and the rose, still quite fresh and fragrant, her face beamed with delight; and Katy went to bed very happy.

The next morning, when Katy reached the store, she found everybody in a state of excitement over the opening of the Christmas goods; for it was but three weeks to Christmas. At the end of the stationery counter, where the pyramid had been, an immense stack of dolls was now attractively displayed. The little cashgirl stood before it, lost in admiration. There were little dolls and big ones; dolls with blue eyes, and others with brown; some with light hair, and some with dark; rubber dolls, and rag dolls with *papier-mache* faces.

"How lovely they are!" she murmured to herself. "I wish Ellie could see them! I'll have to count them, so as to tell her how many there are; for I don't believe that by herself she could imagine such a lot of dolls together."

Katy and Ellie had never had a doll in their lives, that is, a real *boughten* one, as they called those not of home manufacture.

The kind salesgirl who had sent the orange to

Ellie noticed the child's wonderment. After watching her a few moments, Julia called out: "Well, Cash, which do you like best?"

The little girl looked the dolls over again with much deliberation; and finally, pointing to a good-sized one, with golden hair and large eyes, said: "This."

"Oh, one of those ninety-seven cent dolls!" responded Julia. "They *are* handsome for the price. Sawdust bodies, but what fine heads!—red cheeks, splendid eyes, and hair that will comb out as well as that of some costlier ones."

"Ninety-seven cents!" repeated Katy, with a sigh. It was an unattainable sum.

"Why don't you buy it, Cash?" Julia urged. "You wouldn't get such another bargain in a doll if you hunted a year and a day. You'd better speak for it quick, though; for when the rush of customers comes, there's no knowing how long the dolls will last."

Katy shook her head. "I was wishing—only there is really no use in wishing—I was thinking if I could only get that doll for Ellie, how happy she would be. You know she has to be alone so much, and she gets awful blue sometimes; though she won't let on, 'cause it would fret Mother. But the doll would be great company for her. We've neither of us ever had one."

"I'll tell you how you can manage to get it," Julia said, suddenly. "It's the rule of this store that on Christmas Eve, after all the customers are gone, each employee may choose as a present from the firm some article worth a quarter of his or her wages for the week. Let's see: you're paid three dollars, aren't you?"

Katy nodded.

"That would count for seventy-five cents on the doll; then all you would have to put to it would be twenty-two cents. Couldn't you do that somehow?"

"Yes!" cried Katy, delighted. "Sometimes I run errands for a dressmaker who lives in the block below us, and she gives me pennies, or once in a while a nickel. Oh, yes, I'm almost sure I can make up the twenty-two cents! Won't Ellie be happy?"

The tears sprang to the salesgirl's eyes. "After all, love is better than riches," she reflected, as the picture of the crippled child in the humble home arose in her mind.

"You will save this very doll for me, won't you?" pleaded Cash.

"I can't put it aside for you," she explained, "because the floor-manager would not allow that."

"But I want *this* one," declared Katy.

"My goodness gracious, you foolish midget! They're all as much alike as rows of peas in a pod," exclaimed her friend.

"No," insisted the little girl. "All the others have red painted buckles on their shoes, but this doll has blue buckles; and I'm sure Ellie would prefer blue buckles, 'cause we've often talked about it when we played choosing what we'd like best. "

"Well, well," laughed Julia. "All right, Katy: I'll save it, if I can."

Satisfied by this promise, the child ran away to her work.

McNaughton & Co. did a great business within

the next two weeks; the employees were "fearfully rushed," as they expressed it. Katy had been transferred to another department, but every day she went around and looked at the doll, to make sure that it was still there.

One afternoon, however, a few days before Christmas, when Julia returned from her lunch she met Katy, who was crying bitterly. A new girl had been working at the counter that morning; she knew nothing about Katy's doll, and now was just in the act of selling it to a big, bluff-looking man, who said he wanted it for his little daughter.

Julia rushed to her post. The man was upon the point of paying for the doll. "Have you seen the brown-eyed dolls?" Julia interposed, pleasantly. "The brown-eyed ones are considered the most desirable."

"Are they?" the man hesitated. "Well, I believe I'll take one, then, instead of this. My little girl likes brown eyes."

Katy's doll was saved. She turned toward her friend with a face bright with gratitude, as she hurried away in response to the imperative call of "Cash."

Part III

On the morning of the day before Christmas, Katy appeared at the counter with the twenty-two cents—the balance to be paid on her present.

"Can't I take the doll now, please?" she begged.

"You will have to ask the floor-manager," replied Julia.

She did so, but he said she must wait until evening; he could not make any exceptions. So she was obliged to control her impatience.

Scarcely five minutes afterward a crash was heard. The equilibrium of the rack of dolls had been disturbed, and the whole collection was dashed to the floor. Only three or four of the dolls were broken; but, alas! among them was the one Katy had set her heart upon giving to her sick sister.

The commotion brought her to the scene at once. Poor Katy! She did not burst out crying, but clasped her hands and, stood looking at the wreck of the doll, with an expression of hopeless disappointment.

"Don't feel so bad, midget!" Julia whispered, picking up the pieces. "See: only the head is spoiled. There's another doll with the feet knocked off. I'll take the two dolls up to the toy-mender's room, and have the head of the other put on your doll; that will make it as good as new."

She laid the dolls on the shelf behind, and wished that the lady to whom she was showing some very handsome dolls would finish her choice, so that she might get a free minute to run up to the toy-mending room. But the interest of the customer had been awakened by the little drama enacted before her.

"What is the matter?" she inquired, cordially.

The lady had such a sweet and kind face, that the girl found herself telling briefly not only the history of Katy's doll, but of Katy and Ellie too. It was not a waste of time either; for while she talked the purchaser made one or two additional selections, and then, after giving directions concerning them, passed on.

"Do you know who that was?" asked Katy, rushing up as the lady turned into another aisle of the store.

"Yes: Mrs. M——, of 34th Street," replied Julia.

"Oh! my Rose-lady. Don't you remember the one who gave me the pretty flower?" cried the child.

"Why, so it is!" rejoined Julia. "Well, she's a lovely lady certainly. She happened to ask what the trouble was about the doll; and was so interested I couldn't help telling how you had saved and planned to get it for Ellie, and all about it."

"Mercy! did you?" answered the child, in confusion. "My, what would the likes of her care to hear about that!"

The store kept open till half-past eleven Christmas Eve; but at length the employees were allowed to choose their presents. Katy skipped around with joy when the repaired doll was put into her arms. After a moment, however, Julia whisked it away again, and sent it to be packed in a box. The box was large and clumsy, but this was accounted for upon the plea of haste.

"Well, good-night and Merry Christmas, Julia!" said the little cashgirl, gratefully. "I don't know how to thank you enough for being so good and helping me so much!"

"Never mind trying," answered Julia, brightly. "Isn't this Christmas Eve, and didn't the Infant Jesus come to help us, and teach us to do what we can for one another? Just say a prayer for me at Mass tomorrow; that is all I ask."

"You may be sure I will," Katy replied, heartily.

Katy's father was waiting for her at one of the entrances of the store. She allowed him to carry the package, while she trudged along at his side. It was past midnight; in the deep blue of the winter's sky the stars glowed with a peaceful radiance. Looking up at them, Katy began to think of the meaning of Christmas and of Christmas gifts; of the Love that came into the world on that holy night of long ago, to kindle in all hearts a spirit of kindness and helpfulness toward one another, making it more blessed to give than to receive. The little girl realized the happiness of making others happy, when she handed to Ellie the bulky package.

The usually pale face of the young invalid flushed with excitement, while, with trembling fingers, she unfastened the wrappings and opened the box.

"Katy!" she exclaimed, as she beheld the hard-won present— "O Katy!" It was all she could say, but the tone and the look which accompanied it were quite enough.

At first neither of the children could think of anything besides the doll; but after a while Ellie made another discovery. As she trifled with the box, she cried: "Why, there's something else here!"

The next moment she drew out a doll precisely like the first, except that its shoes had red buckles; at the sight of which Katy immediately concluded that, for herself, she liked red buckles better. Attached to it was a card on which was written: "For an unselfish little sister."

"It's for you, Katy," said Ellie, ecstatically.

"Then the Rose-lady must have sent it," declared Katy, feeling as if she were in a dream.

That her conjecture was correct was evident the next day; for about noon a carriage stopped at the door of the dilapidated house; and a visitor, who seemed to bring with her an additional share of Christmas sunshine, was shown up to the Connors' tenement. She was followed by a tall footman, who quietly deposited upon the table a generous basket of the season's delicacies.

"The Rose-lady, Mother!" cried Katy, pinching her own arm to see if she could possibly be awake.

It was all true, however; and that day the Connors family found a devoted friend. Henceforth the Rose-lady took a special interest in Ellie. She induced a celebrated doctor to go and see her. The great man said there was a chance that the crippled child might be cured; and it was arranged that the mother should take her regularly to his office for treatment, Mrs. M—— offering the use of her carriage.

Now Ellie can walk almost as well as ever. She is growing stronger every day, and will probably before long be able to attain her ambition—"to earn money to help Mother."

"And to think, Katy," the little girl often says, affectionately, "it all came about through your wanting to give me that Christmas doll!"

Letters of Recommendation

A gentleman once advertised for a boy to assist him in his office, and nearly fifty applied for the place. Out of the whole number he in a short time chose one, and sent all the rest away.

"I should like to know," said a friend, "on what grounds you chose that boy. He had not a single recommendation with him."

"You are mistaken," said the gentleman, "he had a great many recommendations.

"He wiped his feet when he came in, and closed the door after him; showing that he was orderly and tidy.

"He gave up his seat instantly to that lame old man; showing that he was kind and thoughtful.

"He took off his cap when he came in, and answered my questions promptly and respectfully; showing that he was polite.

"He lifted up the book which I had purposely laid on the floor, and placed it on the table, while all the rest stepped over it, or shoved it aside; showing that he was careful.

"And he waited quietly for his turn, instead of pushing the others aside; showing that he was modest.

"When I talked with him, I noticed that his clothes were carefully brushed, his hair in nice order, and his teeth as white as milk. When he wrote his name, I observed that his fingernails were clean, instead of being tipped with jet, like those of the handsome little fellow in the blue jacket.

"Don't you call these things letters of recommendation? I do; and what I can tell about a boy by using my eyes for ten minutes, is worth more than all the fine letters he can bring me."

The Broken Flowerpot

One fine day in summer, my father was seated on the lawn before the house, his straw hat over his eyes, and his book on his lap. Suddenly a beautiful blue and white flowerpot, which had been set on the windowsill of an upper story, fell to the ground with a crash, and the fragments clattered 'round my father's legs.

"Dear, dear!" cried my mother, who was on the porch. "My poor flowerpot that I prized so much! Who could have done this?" I popped my head out of the window that had been the scene of the accident.

"Oh," said my mother, mournfully, "I would rather have lost all the plants in the greenhouse in the great blight last May; I would rather the best tea set were broken! The poor geranium I grew myself, and the dear, dear flowerpot which you bought for me on my last birthday!"

Coming out of the house as bold as brass, I said in a shrill voice, "I did it, Mama; it was I who pushed out the flowerpot."

My father had very deliberately taken off his hat, and was regarding the scene with serious eyes, wide awake. I suddenly felt very uneasy as his face grew sterner.

"Well," said my mother, "I suppose it was an accident: be more careful in the future, my child. You are sorry, I see, to have grieved me. There is a kiss."

"No, Mamma, you must not kiss me; I don't deserve it. I pushed out the flowerpot on purpose."

"And why?" said my father, walking up. By this time I trembled like a leaf. "For fun," said I, hanging my head; "just to see how you'd look, Papa; and that's the truth of it. Now punish me—do punish me!"

My father threw his book away, stooped down, and caught me to his chest. "Son," he said, "you have done wrong; but remember all your life that your father blessed God for giving him a son who spoke truth in spite of his fear!"

* * * *

Not long after this I received a present of far greater value than are the gifts usually given to children. It was a beautiful, large, ivory domino box. This domino box was my delight. I was never weary of playing dominoes, and I slept with the box under my pillow.

"Ah!" said my father one day, when he found me playing with the ivory pieces. "Ah! you like those better than all your other playthings, eh?"

"Oh, yes, Papa."

"And you would be very sorry if your mother were to throw your box out of the window and break it, for fun?"

I looked at my father, and made no answer.

"But perhaps, you would be very glad," he continued, "if you could change the domino box into a beautiful geranium in a beautiful blue and white flowerpot, that you could have the pleasure of putting it on your mamma's window sill?"

"Indeed I would," said I, wanting to cry.

"My dear boy, I believe you; but good wishes do not mend bad actions—good actions mend bad actions."

So saying, he shut the door and went away. I can not explain just how puzzled I was as I tried to understand what my father meant. But I know I played no more dominoes that day.

The next morning my father found me seated by myself under a tree in the garden; he paused, and looked at me very steadily with his grave, bright eyes.

"My boy," said he, "I am going to walk to town; will you come? And, by the by, fetch your domino box; I would like to show it to a person there."

I ran in for the box, and proud to be walking with my father, I set out with him.

"Papa," said I on the way, "how can my domino box be changed into a beautiful geranium and a blue and white flowerpot?"

"My dear," said my father, leaning his hand on my shoulder, "everybody who is in earnest to be good carries two gifts about with him—one here," and he touched my forehead; "one here," and he touched my heart.

"I don't understand, Papa," said I thoughtfully.

"I can wait until you do, my boy," said he.

My father stopped at a gardener's, and after looking over the flowers, paused before a large double geranium. "Ah, this is finer than the one your mamma was so fond of. What is the price of this, sir?"

"Only seven shillings and sixpence," said the gardener.

My father buttoned up his pocket. "I cannot afford it today," replied my father gently, and he walked out.

On entering the town, we stopped again at a crockery store. "Have you a flowerpot like that I bought some months ago? Ah! Here is one marked three shillings and sixpence. Yes, that is the price. Well, when your mamma's birthday comes again, we must buy her another, my boy. We have yet some months to wait. And we can wait. For truth, which blooms all the year round, is better than a poor flower; and a word that is never broken is better than a piece of china."

"I have called to pay your little bill," said my father, entering one of those stores in which are sold all kinds of things.

"And by the way," he added, as the smiling storekeeper looked over his books for the amount, "I think my little boy here can show you a very handsome specimen of French workmanship. Show your domino box, my dear."

I showed my treasure, and the storekeeper praised it highly. "It is always well, my boy, to know what a thing is worth in case one wishes to part with it. If my son gets tired of his plaything, what will you give him for it?"

"Why, sir," said the shopman, "I fear we could not afford to give more than eighteen shillings for it, unless the young gentleman should take some of these pretty things in exchange."

"Eighteen shillings!" said my father; "you would give that? Well, my boy, whenever you do grow tired of your box, you have my permission to sell it."

My father paid his bill and went out. I lingered behind a bit and then caught up with him at the end of a street.

"Papa, Papa!" I cried, clapping my hands, "we can buy the geranium—we can buy the flowerpot!" And I pulled out a handful of silver from my pockets.

"Was I not right?" said my father, passing his handkerchief over his eyes. "You have found the two gifts of good thoughts and loving deeds!"

Aided by my father, I made the desired purchase, and, on our return, ran into the house. Oh! how proud, how overjoyed I was when, after placing flowerpot and flower on the windowsill, I gently tugged my mother's dress, and made her follow me to the spot. She was speechless with joy when she had learned all.

"It is his doing and his money!" said my father. "Good actions have mended the bad."

The Philosopher and the Boatman

A philosopher, who wished to cross a turbulent stream of water, engaged a boatman to row him over. While on the way, he asked the boatman if he understood algebra.

"Algebra!" exclaimed the boatman, "I never heard of it before. I know nothing about it."

"Then," said the philosopher, "one quarter of your life is lost. But perhaps you know something about metaphysics?"

"Met-a, met-a what?" asked the boatman. "Oh, you wish to know if I ever studied physics. Not much, sir; I have no taste for such things."

"You don't understand me," said the philosopher.

I wished to know whether you have any knowledge of metaphysics—the science which explains the principles and causes of all things existing—psychology."

"I never heard that word before," replied the boatman. "My father was a ferryman, and I have followed the same business ever since I was strong enough to row a boat. I know nothing of Met-a—what do you call it?"

"Well, if you know nothing of metaphysics, then you have lost another quarter of your life. But perhaps you know something about astronomy?" asked the philosopher.

"I know nothing about those things," said the boatman. "I have had other business to attend to."

"Then I must inform you that another quarter of your life is lost. But what is the matter with this boat, and why are you taking off your coat?" asked the philosopher.

"Don't you see," said the boatman, "that the boat has sprung a leak, and is fast sinking? Can you swim?"

"Swim? No, indeed! You don't expect a philosopher like me to swim, do you?"

"Then," said the boatman, "if you can not swim the whole of your life is lost, for the boat is rapidly sinking, and will soon go to the bottom."

"Ah me!" exclaimed the philosopher, "how willingly would I part with all my other knowledge, if by so doing, I could acquire the art of swimming!"

Nina's Trial

"Well, if I can't have Teresa, then I shall not take any name at all." Nina Peyton, facing her classmates, brought her small foot down with a very determined stamp.

"Hush, Nina! Please hush!" said Susie Newton. "Sister Rose will hear you!"

"I hope she will!" returned Nina, perversely. "But I don't intend to lose my Confirmation name, that's all!"

"Oh, hush!" exclaimed two or three voices together, as the door of the classroom opened and Sister Rose entered the classroom.

"What is the matter, children?" she asked, noting at once the air of unusual excitement in the room. "Nina Peyton, why are you out of your seat?"

Nina hung her head, blushed and gave no answer. But there was a naughty, determined expression on her countenance, as she stood there quite still, making no movement toward her seat. Her classmates gazed at her with some apprehension. Surely Nina would not attempt to talk back to Sister Rose!

The nun repeated her question, and now there was something in her voice which compelled obedience.

"Susie Newton says I can't have Teresa for my Confirmation name," replied Nina, speaking very fast. "She says six of the girls have already taken Teresa, and that you don't want any more of us to take it. She has no right to boss me, and I will have the name I want, so there!"

"Nina! Nina!" exclaimed Sister Rose. "Is this the spirit of a child preparing for a great Sacrament?"

"I don't care!" continued Nina—but this time there was an odd little catch in her voice. "I want my St. Teresa."

"And why do you want St. Teresa?" she asked, calmly.

Whatever might be her faults, Nina Peyton was a truthful little girl, and her answer was somewhat startling.

"Because—because—she was such a great, grand saint. She never did small, little things; she always did the big, grand ones. I plan to do something great and high when I grow up, too. Besides—besides, Susie Newton said I couldn't have her."

"My dear," said Sister Rose, reprovingly, "do you think St. Teresa would wish to be the patron of a little girl who chooses her for the reasons you give, especially the last one? Have you ever read the life of St. Teresa, Nina?"

Nina, in honesty, had to answer, "No." She had, however, read the anecdote of the two little Spanish children—the future saint and her brother—running away from home to seek martyrdom at the hands of the Moors. To ambitious little Nina's mind, there was something very enticing in that idea, at least in thought. Since the name of Teresa had not been given her at baptism, she had long hoped to receive it at Confirmation. This is why she was so angry and disappointed when she found her wish might not be possible.

Nina had often been heard to declare her intention of becoming a saint herself some day. She would begin on the very next Monday. It would be fine to fight off big sins, and of course, the little ones weren't worth mentioning. She could conquer them without the slightest trouble. Alas, for poor Nina, how many times had she been obliged to make a fresh start! Sometimes an hour of the day had hardly passed before she had "stopped being a saint," as she expressed it. In each case it wasn't a big fault that had caused the fall, but one of those tiny little things which she so despised. She would either lose her temper because she was contradicted, or speak an uncharitable word, or say something unkind to a companion. Then an uncomfortable feeling would come, and Nina felt she would have to begin all over again next Monday. Why she chose Monday was not quite clear even to Nina, except perhaps that the business of a new week began on that day, and one felt fresher and more like making a new start. Even with her repeated beginnings, and the falls always caused by the little things, Nina could not yet see their immense importance. At least she would not see. It is sad to say, she frequently lost her temper over the very thought that those little things could possibly get the better of her again... We shall return to the discussion between Sister Rose and Nina.

"I thought not," said Sister Rose, when Nina acknowledged she had not read the life. "And I do not advise you to read it yet, my dear child," she continued. "It is a wonderful life, which you would not understand till you are older. But I have read it, children," she went on, now addressing the class, "and let me assure you that if St. Teresa did do great things, she did not by any means despise the perfect doing of little things—the very tiny, ordinary things. For the present, be content to do perfectly the little things around you and before you know it, they will be big things."

Sister Rose paused a minute. Some of the girls looked very thoughtful and serious. Nina's expression was one of doubt.

"Listen," resumed Sister Rose, as she opened a book lying among a few others on her desk. "Hear this: 'It is not what we read in the lives of the saints that make them saints: it is what we do not read of them that enabled them to be what we wonder at while we read.'"

Sister Rose read slowly, and with strong emphasis upon every word. Then she closed the book and looked at Nina. The little girl was repeating the words over to herself. How strange they were!

Presently, before any one had yet spoken, the bell for recreation rang. As the girls were filing out, Sister Rose detained Nina for a few moments. Her manner was very kind and gentle as she said: "Nina, if you desire Teresa for your Confirmation name you may certainly have it. I did request that the children would not all take the same name, as there are many saints in the calendar; and it sometimes happens, that the majority of a class will follow one or two students blindly, like sheep. Susie misunderstood me. You may take whom you choose, provided you are more reverent in future when speaking on such a subject. It is really shocking to think you would quarrel over a saint."

By this time Nina was feeling very repentant and went to the other extreme.

"No, Sister," she said, heroically, "I do not think St. Teresa would want such a person as I am now. I am not worthy. I shall give it up." And Nina had an edified, resigned expression.

"Think it over, dear," answered Sister Rose, smiling a little, "and don't decide too hastily. Remember you have a few weeks yet."

When Nina entered the recreation hall, the girls were talking together very earnestly, but their voices fell to a lower tone as she approached.

"Don't ask her to join; she despises such things," said somebody in a whisper just loud enough for Nina to hear.

"Oh, yes, I will!" replied Susie Newton, who was evidently the ruling spirit. "I wouldn't start up a club without Nina, though we do have little quarrels now and then."

On hearing the remark of the first girl, Nina was about to turn away in high disdain, but Susie's manner and the mention of a club stopped her.

"Want to join the C. L. T. Club?" asked Susie. "It is a secret club, Nina, and it will be such fun! Come on, help make up the rules." And Susie hospitably made room for her on the bench beside her. "You see," she explained, pointing to a paper before her, while a number of eager heads were craned over her shoulder, "C.L.T.C. means Conquer Little Things Club. It just came into my head to start it while Sister Rose was talking. As soon as we get all the rules made up we'll elect a president and design our badges. It will just be so special," continued Susie, becoming more fired up with her idea. "My brothers and all the boys I know belong to clubs, and they're so awfully mysterious about them. How inquisitive they'll be when they see our badges!"

"But go on, Susie, go on with the rules," suggested somebody.

Thus adjured, Susie began to read from the paper before her. Her tone was very important, as befitting such solemn words:

"Whereas, I hereby vow and resolve on this 20th day of April, in the year of Our Lord 1889, that to the uttermost of my power and ability; whereas, I will comply with the following rules and regulations governing the C. L. T. C.; whereas, resolved, the following rules: Rule one" —

But here somebody interrupted. "My! How could you make it sound so nice and law-ish, Susie?"

"My big brother is going to be a lawyer," announced Susie.

This explanation was enough, and the girls listened with awe at Susie's legal knowledge.

"Go on," said Nina, eagerly. Evidently this was interesting.

"Well, then. Rule One: Don't lose your temper even if people say the smallest, meanest things to you. Rule Two: If people ever make fun of you, don't let them see you care. Rule Three: Don't give a sharp answer, even to the crankiest person in the world. Rule Four: When you feel you are dying for some candy, just conquer your desire and give the money to the poor. Rule Five: Don't insist on people listening to your opinion, give in gently. Rule six: Don't quarrel. Rule Seven: If you have little sisters and brothers, tell them stories when they ask, even when you feel like enjoying a quiet time of reading; and if there's a baby in your family, and you are caring for it, be gentle even when it squeals."

Here Susie paused. "That's all I could think of so far," she said. "Perhaps it's enough. They'll be hard to keep, though they sound easy."

"I don't think so," said Nina, decidedly. "Of course, some of them sound silly enough, but dear me! We can easily do all those things if we make up our minds to it. I think we ought to have a few more rules—really hard ones; there won't be any glory in keeping those tiny things."

"Well, this isn't going to be a club for conquering grand things," replied Susie. "If it proves a success at the end of the week, then you may make up something of that kind."

Nina reluctantly agreed, and the girls, all very much interested, went about electing a president. Of course, the choice fell upon Susie, who blushingly accepted the honor. Each girl was to make her own badge that evening at home; the badges were to be of white ribbon, embroidered with the mystic letters of the club in gold.

After school that afternoon they went together to a little toyshop, where every girl bought herself a small box containing one hundred common black beads. Each time a member broke one of the rules she was to slip one of these beads on a string. At the end of the week the girl who had the least number on her string was to be crowned with flowers—

paper ones would do, Susie explained—and become president the following week. The girl who had strung the greatest number of black beads was to wear a piece of black ribbon over her badge as a sign of disgrace during the following week. And the club was to begin from that very minute, according to the wish of Susie, who, unlike Nina, never thought it necessary to wait until Monday to make a fresh start.

As Nina walked home she entertained two pleasant thoughts: one was that she would probably be the president for the coming week, the other, how very becoming the crown of flowers would be to her. Once or twice however, what Sister Rose had said and read crossed her mind, and it made her feel slightly uncomfortable. Perhaps Sister Rose had been mistaken, though; and Nina thought she could prove her wrong. By the end of the week, Nina had proven something. Let's follow her home to see what it was.

The girls had copied the rules on separate slips of paper, and our Nina was reading hers over with a scornful smile as she neared home. Suddenly her hat shot swiftly over her eyes; then somehow she was tripping over someone else's foot. And the next instant she found herself sitting on the front door mat—surely a ridiculous position in front of the many pedestrians and occupants of vehicles who were passing by on the crowded street. At the same moment, a shout of boyish laughter attested to somebody's enjoyment over the success of his trick. Tommy, the most mischievous of her small brothers, surrounded by three pals of his own size, stood looking at her with amazing glee from the safe position they had taken.

Without an instant's hesitation, her eyes flashing with anger, Nina turned on her brother. Of course, he had anticipated this, and all four made their escape with surprising ease. Nina chased them for a block or more, but at last realized that their head start would not allow her to catch them. Very much ruffled and disordered looking, she returned to the house, vowing she would have Tommy well punished for what he had done.

"Oh Nina, your hair's all coming loose! What's the matter?" asked her sweet little sister on meeting her in the hall.

"Move out of the way, and let me upstairs!" exclaimed Nina crossly.

As she reached the upper landing her mother appeared with the baby in her arms.

"Hold the baby a moment, dear," she said, "I hear your papa calling me." Nina would have refused if she dared. As it was, the poor baby, who was unusually fussy that day, received more impatient rocking in the next three minutes than he ever had before. And as each rock only increased his cries, Nurse was sure he was going to have a fit when finally she appeared and claimed him.

Nina darted away to her own room, shut the door and locked it. Then she sat down and tried to spread out the slip of paper, now considerably crumpled, on the small dressing table before her.

"Good gracious, me!" she exclaimed suddenly, as her eyes fell upon the words at the head of the page, "Don't lose your temper..."—"but I've broken a rule already!" Poor Nina almost dropped out of her chair in her amazement. Again her eyes wandered to the paper, and again she read: "Rule Two—and I've broken that, too! But—but how could I help it? Oh, those horrid, horrid boys, to make me break two rules all at once!"

It was very hard, but Nina found courage to go on. She discovered that she had also broken the third—spoken so crossly to her little sister. Then with resignation she decided to find out how many more she had broken.

Rules Four and Five were "all right" she found. "Rule Six: Don't quarrel. Haven't broken that yet," said Nina aloud, "but I will when I catch Tom. I wasn't gentle with the baby; of course, that means I broke the seventh rule. Oh, dear me! What shall I do?"

The most practical thought that suggested itself was the stringing of her black beads. She took the box out of her pocket, feeling very discouraged indeed, and proceeded to count out five black ones. "Though I only broke four really; still I suppose I'll break that 'Don't quarrel' one," she explained to herself. "But," she added suddenly catching the fifth bead and pulling it off again, "no, I won't. I'll make a fresh start from this minute, I'll let Tom off this time."

Then she proceeded to arrange her hair and dress before appearing downstairs again. She had immense faith in herself still, and certainly, she was not going to lose courage over four black beads.

At the dinner table that evening, Tommy was the last to make his appearance. When he did come in he slipped hastily into his place, glancing from under a pair of twinkling eyes at Nina. But Nina was serene and gracious to an extraordinary degree. Tommy's courage went up like mercury in a thermometer suddenly brought from a cold room into one greatly heated.

"I say, Nina," he began, sidling up to his sister a little later, "want some daisy candy?"

Nina was not by any means above sweets, and accepted Tom's reparation at once.

"Good, isn't it?" said the boy, regarding her with great interest as she tasted the morsel.

"It's fine!" agreed Nina. "But where did you get it, Tom?"

"In that new store round on the avenue," was the answer. "And, gee, but it's dandy cheap, two pounds for a quarter!"

"Really!" exclaimed the little girl incredulously. "Why Tom, it is almost as good as Hunter's second quality."

"You bet!" agreed Tommy.

"I wish I had some more," said Nina as she finished the enticing morsel. "I feel so much like enjoying some candy tonight."

"I'll go buy you some," answered her small brother willingly. "Get two pounds, Nina. It's only a quarter, you know."

Nina opened her purse; she had just twenty-five cents remaining of her monthly allowance. A shadow suddenly darkened the dining-room window near which the two were sitting, and a timid knock sounded at the basement door. Cook opened it, muttered, "Be off at once!" and then slammed it quickly again. "Nothing but pestering beggars!" Then two barefoot little boys slowly passed the window again and were lost to sight in the dim street.

"Jane is an old crank. She should have given those poor children something," remarked Nina, indignantly.

"Come on, give me the money," said Tommy, uninterestedly, "it's getting late."

Nina drew it forth—at the same time, her paper with the list of rules fell on the floor. She picked it up quickly, and it then flashed across her mind that she was about to break another rule: "Rule Four: When you feel like you are dying for some candy, just conquer your desire, and give the money to the poor." Two beggars had just appeared, and she had let them go empty-handed.

"Well, but that wasn't my fault," Nina consoled herself. "It was that stingy old Jane's fault. I never thought."

And now that the beggars were really gone, Tommy might as well get the candy, it wasn't likely any others would come that night. And he did get the candy, the wonderful candy that was going for such a bargain. Nina consoled herself by sharing it generously with all the children, though the consequences proved rather disastrous; for Mother and Nurse were up nearly all night administering medicines to the younger ones who had eaten too much of it.

Poor Nina herself felt wretched the following morning. She sat in the classroom feeling very miserable and dejected, partly the effect of the candy and the dose of medicine, and partly from the knowledge that her string held the largest number of black beads. She had broken the rules seven times the evening before, and four times again before starting for school that morning. Nina was five black beads ahead of any other member of the Club.

For the first time, it began to dawn upon Nina that she had allowed the little things to conquer her all her life. The truth was a very unpleasant one, and yet it was staring her in the face. Nina, knowing she had more beads than the others, felt herself growing to be a very humbled, heartbroken little girl. On the morning of the fifth day her box was empty, her string was full. Then she broke down altogether.

"Never mind, dear," said Susie Newton, with her arms tightly clasped around her, while the others looked on compassionately. "We know it's harder for you because you happen to have difficulty with every one of the rules, and you never could see the use of thinking of the little things."

"But I tried very, very hard this week," sobbed Nina. "I didn't ever think I'd try so with little things, and now it hasn't been a bit of use."

"Yes, it has," said Sister Rose gently, who had broken in upon the group, and to whom the secret of the Club had, of course, been confided. "Poor child," she continued, softly stroking Nina's hair, "it has taught you golden lessons in humility, and the folly of trusting to your own strength even in conquering those troublesome little things. My Nina is a much better child today than she was a week ago."

"I never felt more wicked in my life, Sister," said Nina, lifting a very tear-stained face. "I don't think there's a worse person in the world. It doesn't seem any use to try any more." Nina did look very dejected.

"Courage, Nina, courage!" said Sister brightly. "Try again and don't lose heart even if you do fail. It is much harder to be patient with ourselves than to be so with others."

Two weeks later Nina took her place in the procession of white-veiled girls about to be confirmed. Her card bore the name of Teresa. Sister Rose had insisted upon that. But it was a trembling, contrite and humble little heart that Nina offered to her great patron.

Honesty Rewarded

Jean Baptiste Colbert, a boy of fifteen, was busy arranging the rolls of cloth in the shop, when Mr. Certain, who was both his employer and godfather, called him, and said: "I want you to take these pieces of cloth to the hotel to Mr. Cenani, the banker from Paris, who is staying there. The prices, with samples attached, are on these tickets, and you must be careful not to make a mistake."

"Am I to take any less than the prices marked?" asked Jean.

"Not a sou," answered the man. "You are to get the full price, and be sure to bring back the money with you."

Accompanied by a porter, who carried the cloth, Jean went to the hotel, and was shown to Mr. Cenani's room. The banker carefully examined the several pieces of cloth, and putting one aside, said, "I like this best. How much is it?"

"Fifteen crowns a yard," answered Jean. The porter smiled at this, but neither Jean nor the banker noticed him.

"This will do," said Mr. Cenani. "Give me thirty yards of it. I want it for hangings for my library."

While Jean and the porter measured the cloth, the banker walked carelessly to his desk, and taking from it a roll of gold, counted out four hundred and fifty crowns, which he handed to Jean. The lad then wrote a receipt for the money. This done, he and the porter departed.

"Well," said Mr. Certain, as the two entered the shop, "did you make a sale? How did you succeed? You've made no mistake, I hope?"

"I don't think I have, sir," answered Jean quietly.

"But I do," said the porter, laughing.

"Ah! I might have expected it," cried the merchant, as he hurried to examine the cloth. "But I give you fair notice, you shall pay for your blunder."

"Don't be uneasy," said the porter. "The mistake is in your favor. He sold for fifteen crowns a yard a cloth marked only six."

The merchant's manner changed at once. "Ah! good boy," he said. "That's the way to make mistakes. Fifteen crowns for a six-crown cloth! What a splendid profit! Jean, my dear boy, I am proud of you. You will be a great man."

For a moment Jean could not speak, so astonished was he. But when he recovered from his surprise, "Godfather," cried he, "you surely would not take advantage of this mistake? It is not honest and I, at least, shall take no part in it. I shall go at once to Mr. Cenani, and return the money he has overpaid." And before the merchant was fairly aware of it, the lad was out of the store, and on his way to the banker.

Rare Catholic Stories

When Jean reached the hotel, he went at once, without being announced, to Mr. Cenani's room, and in answer to the call "Come in," entered. The banker looked surprised and displeased. "What do you want?" he asked. "I cannot be disturbed now, I am engaged. Come some other time."

"Ah, sir!" said the boy, "pardon me, but I must speak to you. By mistake I overcharged you on the cloth you bought, and I come to return you your money," and he laid the gold pieces on the table.

"But you might have kept the money for yourself," said Mr. Cenani, who seemed to forget his hurry, and was now quite interested.

"I never thought of that," answered Jean.

"But if you had thought of it?"

"I could not think of such a thing. It would not be honest," answered the smiling boy.

"You are a fine fellow," said Mr. Cenani, and then asking the boy's name, and inquiring about his family, he dismissed him with the remark, "We shall meet again, Jean, we shall meet again."

On his return to the shop, Jean was met by his godfather, who was in a towering passion. "So this is your gratitude," he cried, as the boy entered, "for all that I have done for you! Leave my sight, and never let me lay eyes on you again." Jean made no answer, but sorrowfully turned his steps homeward. His parents were poor, and, small as his wages were, they would miss the sum, so it was with a heavy heart that he entered the house.

His parents were astonished to see him at that unusual hour. He told, as simply as possible, what had happened, and when he had done, added, "I know not what to do, but I must not remain here idle, a burden on you."

For answer, his mother embraced him warmly, while his father, grasping his hand, said, "Tomorrow we can think of that; today we must think only how we can entertain the noble guest whom Heaven has sent us. For you have acted nobly, my son, and I am, indeed, proud of you."

In the midst of this touching family scene, Mr. Cenani was shown into the room. "I must apologize for this intrusion," he said, "but I leave for Paris early in the morning, and felt that I must see you before going. I have been witness to your son's honesty, and have since learned that by it he lost his situation. I have come, therefore, to offer him a position in our banking-house where we need just such lads as he."

Jean, who had listened in silence to so much praise, his face covered with blushes, now stepped forward. "I am deeply obliged to you, sir," he said, "but my father and mother need me, and as I cannot leave them, I must decline your generous offer."

"But I do not decline it," said his father, tenderly but seriously. "We are very poor, my son. Go, Jean, with this gentleman; in all that concerns the business of your calling, listen to his advice, and follow it; when the principles of integrity and of honor are involved, add to his counsels those of your own heart."

Jean served the banking-house faithfully and well; and, whilst serving it, obtained that complete knowledge of business and finance which afterwards enabled him to be so useful a servant of the State.

In 1661 he was made Minister of Finance to Louis XIV. On his appointment to the office, he found bribery and cheating going on on all sides, and the State yearly robbed of millions of crowns. To the difficult task of reforming these shameless abuses, he brought, with extraordinary abilities and energy, the same courageous and unbending truthfulness which had distinguished him as a boy.

The Heart of the King

When Father Clark returned from his vacation, he was informed that the beautiful mansion next to the rectory had been sold and was now occupied by a non-Catholic family.

One afternoon while the pastor was reading in the garden, he was amused to hear a child's voice administering a lecture to her dog. "You are a bad, bad dog, Rover, for you have broken my dollie's arm!"

The priest watched the scene and smiled at the pretty picture made by the beautiful child and the St. Bernard dog. Seeing him smile, the little maid came to the fence and, thrusting the doll through the bars, she asked, "Mister, please mend my doll?" The Father took the maimed doll and saw that he could remedy the misfortune with the aid of adhesive plaster.

"I shall have to take your dollie into the house for a little while," remarked the priest.

"I must go, too," the child answered. The nurse was approaching, and the Father asked if there would be any objection. The nurse lifted her charge over the fence, and soon Father Clark was busy with the afflicted doll, while her owner watched closely.

"What is your name?" asked the priest.

"When I am good, I am Evelyn but when I am naughty, I am called Eve." Father Clark laughed.

"What is your name?" the little one asked.

"When I am good, I am named Father James but when I am naughty, people call me Father Jim."

Evelyn clapped her hands and said, "I am glad you are naughty, too."

The next day, while reading his Office in the garden, the Father heard Evelyn call, "Father James!" but, as he wished to finish the psalm, he did not answer. Again she repeated his name; still no reply. Then at last a shrill, little voice called, "Father Jim!" Surely this could not be resisted and Father Clark approached the fence where Evelyn stood with her hands behind her back. "You were naughty," she admonished, "but I have a present for you because you cured my dollie, and I like you, too." She handed him a beautiful, red rosebud. The priest thanked the child and told her that he would give it to his Best Friend.

"Where does your Best Friend live?"

"Over there," he said, pointing to the church.

"Bring me to see Him?"

At this moment Evelyn's mother came from the house and, approaching the Father, remarked that she hoped that the child was not annoying him. Father Clark heartily responded that he loved little children and never tired of having them around. Permission was given for Evelyn to come to the Rectory as often as the Father wished. So the child had the opportunity of paying her first visit to the church.

Father Clark placed the rose in a vase and lifted the little one up so that she might come closer to the beautiful statue of the Sacred Heart. "Poor Best Friend!" murmured Evelyn. "Father James, won't you cure His Hands and Feet as you did my dollie's?" The priest told the child of the Loving Heart that wished to suffer because people were bad.

"I shall bring Best Friend a nice rose every day to make Him happy." Evelyn kept her promise, and the Heart that loves little children was comforted each day by a visit from the child.

One morning Evelyn did not appear, and her father, Mr. Trevett, called on Father Clark, bearing a beautiful bunch of roses. "Evelyn is ill but she made me promise that I would bring you a rose, Father. Will you please come when you are at leisure and assure her that I have kept my word?"

Father Clark called to see his little friend and found her very ill. He asked the parents to allow him to baptize the child and they readily agreed. When he had finished, Evelyn whispered, "Father James, tell Best Friend I shall come tomorrow."

The next evening, when the nurse had left the room, Evelyn climbed from her bed and, taking a white rose from a vase on the table, stole out of the house to the church. Father Clark was praying before the altar, when he saw the child totter through the sacristy door to the statue of the Sacred Heart. Before the priest could reach her, she fell, still clinging to the flower. Gently the Father lifted the child he loved so dearly, but her Best Friend Whose love was greater still, had taken her soul to rest within His Divine Heart.

During the lonely months that followed, Mr. and Mrs. Trevett came to know the Heart of Jesus and to receive comfort from Him as their Best Friend.

The Countersign

One fine moonlit night, during a late war in Europe, a lonely sentinel was pacing up and down his solitary beat when, suddenly, he heard a faint sound, like that of a stealthy footstep. It came from a clump of trees which formed the boundary to a portion of the land occupied by the camp.

He at once concluded that someone was trying to enter secretly, and so moved forward to the spot just as a man in uniform came into view.

Loud and clear rang the sentry's voice, as placing

himself in front of the stranger he spoke the usual words at such a time: "Who goes there?"

"A friend," was the feebly uttered answer.

"Advance, friend, and give the countersign."

I ought to explain here to my young readers, that, in time of war, soldiers are every night placed at regular distances from each other, on all sides of the camp, to act as watchmen, and are forbidden under pain of death to permit any one to pass them in any direction, unless sent by an officer.

To make sure of this, a word or two, or a sign, is chosen every night by the officers, which none know but their own men and the sentinels. This is called the countersign. Of course, any one who does not know the countersign is considered to be an enemy.

When the sentinel said, "Advance! and give the countersign," the stranger replied, "I do not know it. If I did, I would not have tried to enter secretly; but do you not see by my dress that I am one of you? Three months I pined in the enemy's prison; yesterday, I escaped. Let me pass, for the love of God. I am ready to die with fatigue."

The sentry shuddered, for he was a devout Catholic, and his heart ached to have to refuse this request. Besides, he believed the stranger was speaking the truth.

Still his orders were to shoot any one who attempted to enter the camp without giving the countersign. "You have broken our rule," he said, sorrowfully. "You have broken it, and the punishment is death."

"I am not fit to die," said the other, in a hoarse voice. "I have offended God grievously in the past; I must have time to repent before death."

"I give you five minutes to pray."

The young man sank upon his knees, raised his eyes to heaven, and made the sign of the cross.

"You are saved!" cried the sentry, "because of our Holy Faith. The Sign of the Cross is the counter-sign tonight."

Pollie's Five Dollars

Part I

"A happy birthday, Pollie! A happy birthday!" cried the Tyrell children one morning, as that little girl appeared for breakfast.

"Why, is it possible!" exclaimed their father, and regarding her in pretended surprise, as if the important fact had entirely escaped his memory. "And, let me think—how old is my second daughter?" he added reflectively. "Why, she must be eleven, I declare!" he continued, with well-feigned astonishment and a merry twinkle in his eye.

"Twelve, Papa!" corrected Pollie, anxious to assert the dignity of her dozen years. That Papa should not remember was really too bad, she thought.

"Well, ah! 'tis indeed so! My dear, what shall we do about it?" he asked, smiling, putting his hand in his pocket.

All the children looked expectant. Gertrude, the eldest, secure in the superior wisdom of a clever person of fourteen years, smiled knowingly. Rob, who was "half-past ten," as he said, became intensely interested, and relieved his feelings by kicking the shins of his brother John under the table, as a signal to that young hopeful to watch what was coming. John scowled, and retaliated by slyly sprinkling salt, instead of sugar, over the saucer of oatmeal he was passing to Rob. Toosie was staring in round-eyed wonder, waiting to see what Papa was going to do.

"Well, Mary," said Papa, dropping the nickname of endearment, and addressing her with mock ceremony, "I suppose, as you have grown so old and sensible, you may be trusted to spend *this* wisely."

And taking out a crisp, new, five dollar note, he put it into the hands of the delighted Pollie, who for a moment was in such a whirl of exultation and surprise, that she could not even thank him.

"O Papa, how good you are!" exclaimed Pollie, jumping up, and giving him a kiss.

Her father laughed, and patted her braid of soft hair as he rose to go to work. Then, with a pleasant nod to them all, he was off.

"Crickey, that's a jolly present!" exclaimed Rob, much impressed.

Baby Toosie "did not see why Pollie should make such a fuss about a scrap of paper, even if it *had* a pretty picture on it." Gertrude appeared almost as pleased as Pollie herself.

"It *is* very nice of Papa, isn't it, Mamma?" said Pollie effusively.

"Yes, truly," assented Mrs. Tyrell, who, however, wondered if it had been an altogether wise thing to do. Pollie was so careless. But she only added: "Don't disappoint Papa's confidence in you, dear. Be careful not to lose your money; and, in thinking of what you will do with it, remember that to try to make others happy is the surest way to be happy ourselves."

"Of course, Mamma," answered the little girl.

"Mamma doesn't seem to realize that I am growing up!" she complained to Gertrude, as the sisters went out on the porch. And Pollie, who was already as tall as her stately little mother, held her head erect, and felt that she was quite competent to take care of her newly-acquired fortune, or to dispose of it, without suggestions from anyone.

Part II

The two girls were an attractive picture as they stood near the porch. Gertrude was of dark complexion, with a profusion of glossy brown hair, laughing gray eyes, and a merry dimpled face. Gertrude dearly loved fun and frolic; she liked to be neatly dressed, but cared nothing for style or fashion. Pollie, on the contrary, was already looking forward to the time when she should leave school, and have something to say about the way her dresses should be made. She was fair, and had a thick braid of red-gold hair; she always looked trim and daintily costumed.

As a birthday present, Gertrude had given Pollie a pretty embroidered handkerchief. The latter was examining it, and her five-dollar note, with a gratified expression, when Rob ran up to them with a message:

"Girls! Alice and Kittie Morton, and several others, are over at the tennis-court. They want to know if you'll go and have a game?"

"Indeed we will!" cried Gertrude, ever ready for any amusement which promised exercise in the open air. Pollie hastily tucked the money and the handkerchief into her pocket, and followed her sister to the court.

The boys concluded to go a-fishing. They secured bait, took up their position on the bank of the stream nearby, and while waiting for a bite, settled many grave questions to their own satisfaction, after the manner of older anglers. An hour or two passed, during which they had succeeded in catching a few minnows.

"I say, Rob!" remarked John, casually, "It's good for all of us that Papa gave Pollie such a scrumptious present. Now she'll be sure to have something grand for her *fête*."

"That's so!" replied Rob, at once falling in with his brother's train of thought.

"Let's go and look for her, she must have finished playing tennis; and try to find out what she is going to do for that day," proposed mischievous John.

"All right!" responded Rob. And, hiding their fishing-poles among the bushes, they scampered toward the house.

Pollie's *fête* was one of the principal festivals of the year, in the Tyrell family. Her birthday was the 2nd of September; but, beyond the presentation of gifts, it was not celebrated till the 8th, the Feast of the Birth of Our Lady. When about five years old she was very ill. Her mother prayed to Our Lady, to obtain that her life might be spared if 'twere God's will, and, on this day the child was pronounced out of danger by the doctors. Thereafter, the beautiful feast was kept with gladness and rejoicing by the entire household. Usually, they had a little family garden party, Papa took them upon an excursion, or some other amusement was provided. And then, in honor of the day, and because every one seemed intent upon making her happy, Pollie considered it a privilege to be allowed to distribute among them a few simple gifts.

These were generally the work of her own deft fingers; but sometimes, if she had saved any pocket money, she would add a trifle or two bought at the toy store. But now Pollie had five dollars; and the boys agreed that she could afford to be generous, and still have something left for herself.

Meantime, tennis proved particularly fascinating. The exercise was heating, and Pollie took much satisfaction in fluttering her pretty handkerchief and fanning herself with it, thus displaying it to advantage. After the game, Gertrude walked part of the way home with the Morton girls, but Pollie decided to go indoors and read. As she was passing through the hall, she suddenly thought of her five dollars. Conscious of negligence, she plunged her hand into her pocket in search of it. But, alas! it did not seem to be there. In alarm, she drew out the handkerchief, but in vain: it was not there. She turned the pocket inside out; looked around on the floor: all without avail. The five-dollar note was gone!

Part III

Poor Pollie! Her heart sank in consternation, a queer lump came in her throat, and the pretty handkerchief was needed to wipe away tears of mortification and regret. Then she started up; slowly retraced her steps across the lawn, along the road to the tennis-court, eagerly scanning every foot of the way, seeking her lost treasure. All was useless, and the foolish girl shrank from telling her mother. Mamma never said "I told you so," but Pollie felt she deserved a reproof for having been so extremely careless.

"Oh, well!" she reflected, "it is not necessary to tell anyone at present, perhaps I may find it after all." Thus, trying to take comfort by looking at the bright side, she went into the house to dinner.

During the meal, Mamma chatted so pleasantly and kindly, treating her as if she were now old enough to be regarded as a companion, that if they had been alone Pollie would certainly have confided in her. As it was, she felt very much ashamed of herself. Gertrude came in late, but atoned for her tardiness by narrating a funny experience she had met with on the way home, and set them in high glee. Pollie felt the dear girl was trying to make her birthday pass as merrily as possible.

"Ah! if she only knew!" sighed our heroine, disconsolately, after laughing at one of her sister's lively sallies.

"I say, Pollie!" cried irrepressible John, "I suppose you will treat us to something worthwhile for your *féte* this year."

The little girl flushed and did not answer. Mrs. Tyrell gave him an admonitory look.

"Well, Pollie," volunteered Rob, avoiding his mother's efforts to catch his eye, "if it's all the same to you, you need not buy anything for us. Just chip in something toward the new bicycle we are saving up for. We've got fifty cents already."

Everyone laughed at the amount of the fund.

From that time, poor Pollie's life was a burden. Not having at first simply acknowledged that she had lost her money, she could not bring herself to do so later. And everybody appeared so eager to help her to spend it. The boys, little rogues, were continually offering suggestions, having found that any allusion to the subject teased her. Papa joked her a good deal about her fortune, and pretended to be curious to know how she intended to invest it. Gertrude thought 'twas very strange that Pollie always dismissed with disfavor any plan for the *fête* which would seem to call, even remotely, for the least expenditure on her part. And Mamma could not understand why her daughter refused to heed a word of counsel to try to do a little good by bestowing a small share in charity.

At last came the day of the *fête*. The children evidently hoped Pollie had a grand surprise in store for them. Instead, the occasion found the disconsolate child but ill prepared; for she had intended to purchase most of her gifts this year, and had hinted to papa that a present of money would be most acceptable on her birthday. Now, therefore, the petty trifles which she hastily collected made but a sorry array.

The boys did not hesitate to express their disgust

when each received a pin ball; and Toosie complained that she did not like paper dolls.

It was rather late in the year to give Papa a calendar, and Mamma a sachet bag—both of which she had herself received at Christmas; and Gertrude could not help looking hurt when she received the remnant of a box of note-paper—Pollie knew "she could not bear to write letters."

So, unhappy Pollie, after doing the best she could, had the dissatisfaction of knowing she had not succeeded in pleasing anyone; for even Papa opened his eyes wider than usual, and Mamma's face wore a grieved, troubled expression, as if she feared her little girl was growing selfish. That afternoon, Papa was to take them all for a long drive to Greenwood Lake, where they were to have a picnic. Pollie was helping Mamma to pack the baskets, when Gertrude came back from a trip to the village.

"O Mamma and Pollie!" said she, "Kitty Morton has such a splendid idea. She proposes that we girls should present a pair of handsome vases to the Blessed Virgin's altar in the church here, in honor of Our Lady's birthday. All of our friends are going to give something, and Mrs. Morton is going to town and will buy them today. I told Kitty I would come home and get all the pocket money I had saved, and I was sure Pollie would be generous, because this is her special *fête*." She glanced confidently toward her sister.

"I do not see why you should be so ready to say what I will do!" cried Pollie, crossly.

Gertrude, quite taken aback, paused and gazed at her in amazement; then silently left the room. Mrs.

Tyrell was also astonished. After a moment, as Pollie offered no explanation, she said quietly:

"I hope my daughter is not becoming niggardly. It is well to be prudent and economical, dear, yet the best use of money is not to hoard, but to expend it in doing good, and making others happy. See how ready Gertrude is to give what she has for Our Lady's shrine; if you are unwilling to do anything, how can you expect a blessing on your *féte*?"

Pollie burst into tears.

"Indeed, Mamma," faltered she, "I am not a little miser, as the boys called me this morning. The truth is I lost my money."

"Lost it!" echoed Mrs. Tyrell, almost doubting if she had heard aright. "Why, when, pray?"

"On my birthday—right away—before dinner!" sobbed Pollie.

"Well, well! You poor child!" said her mother sympathetically. So Pollie told the whole story. When she had finished, Mrs. Tyrell said:

"I shall not make any remarks about it, my daughter, for you have been well punished for your negligence, and this experience has taught you a lesson which you are not likely to forget."

"But don't tell any one! Will you, Mamma?" pleaded Pollie.

"I think it would be much better to say frankly that you lost your money," replied Mrs. Tyrell. "I dislike family misunderstandings. Still, this is your own affair. I shall not mention it, and you must do as you think best."

Part IV

Time went on. Before long Pollie had confided her secret to Gertrude. After awhile, she suspected that Papa had guessed it. But, though the boys continued to twit her, and to call her little miser, she would not condescend to set herself right with them; and her mother did not interfere, thinking that if Pollie was too proud to acknowledge her fault, she ought to bear the penalty.

One day in November, after the family had returned to the city, Mrs. Tyrell, in looking over the children's clothes, came upon Pollie's brown gown.

"I think, dear, you have outgrown this," said she. "If you wish, you may give it to little Maggie Cronin; it will help to make her comfortable this winter."

Pollie readily assented, and thus, the dress found its way into a bundle which Widow Cronin, the washerwoman, was told to take home with her.

On a certain afternoon shortly after, Pollie chanced to go into the kitchen, where she found Maggie, who had just asked to see her. The latter was a gentle little girl, a year younger than Pollie.

"Mother sent me to tell you about that brown dress," she said at once.

"Why, what about it?" asked Pollie. "Didn't you like it?"

"Oh, yes!" answered Maggie, hastily. "But it had to be made over. It was lined, you know."

"Well?" observed Pollie, wishing that Maggie would hurry with what she had to say.

"When I had ripped a little way—right between the skirt and the lining I found this," said Maggie, holding up before their eyes *the lost five dollars!*

"Oh!" gasped Pollie, too bewildered to say more, as she gazed in fascination on the treasure-trove, which the little girl still clutched firmly, as if loath to give it up.

"You don't know how happy I was when I found it," continued Maggie wistfully, speaking as if something were choking her. "Mother was out washing, and I thought how glad she would be. And then I began to plan about all the things I would buy with it—a warm shawl for mother, because her old one is getting so thin; and shoes and stockings for Biddeen and little Jim; they haven't any, so they can't go out, and their feet look so blue and cold. And for Pat, too; besides a suit of clothes for him to wear to school. And, oh! A pair of blankets and some coal! And then—" Maggie stopped and looked confused, as if she felt she had been very foolish;— "then, with what was left, I just thought I should like to buy a bit of red wing for my Sunday hat. I suppose I was silly, but they are only ten cents apiece at Brown's, and one would brighten up the hat so that it would not look so shabby. You know," she added, "poor girls like pretty things, as well as rich girls."

Pollie was touched. "But Maggie," she said, "you never could get all that for five dollars."

"Couldn't I?" asked the other in surprise. "Anyhow, it does not make any difference now," she continued, with a little sigh. "When Mother came home, I showed her the bill, and told her all I was going to do with it. Already I could see mother wearing the warm shawl, the shoes and stockings on the children, and Pat dressed in his new suit; even"—here Maggie's voice trembled, though she smiled— "the little red feather in my hat. And I did not seem to notice then, but I remembered afterward, that all the time, Mother never spoke, only kept looking at me, as if she were sorry to have to disappoint me. At last she said: 'But the money is not yours, Maggie.'—'To be sure it is!' says I. 'Didn't Miss Pollie Tyrell give it to me?'—'Not the money,' says she.—'Didn't she give me the dress, and wasn't the money in the dress?' answers I.—'Yes, but she didn't know it was there, Maggie dear,' says Mother. 'She didn't mean to give it to you, and it would not be honest to keep it.'

"And she made me come right up with it to you. So take it, Miss Pollie Tyrell!" cried Maggie tearfully, thrusting the bank-note into Pollie's hands, and running away, as if afraid she might be tempted to snatch it back again.

Pollie stood looking at it, as if she could not believe her eyes. Was this really the five dollar note which she had lost so long before? "Ah!" she reflected, "I think I understand how it happened. There was a tear in the dress near the pocket. That morning in my hurry, I must have slipped the money in there, instead of into the pocket." Having decided this point in her own mind, she went upstairs and carefully locked the bill away in her work-box. "How fortunate I am," she thought. "I shall not tell any one but Mamma about the way it was found. But now, I can show everybody that I am not stingy. I shall buy a nice present for each member of the family, even for the boys, though they have plagued me so."

Mrs. Tyrell was as much surprised as Pollie anticipated when she heard the circumstances of Maggie Cronin's visit, and the sequel to the history of the five dollars. Yet Pollie felt that, somehow, her mother did not enter quite heartily into her project for disposing of it.

"I may spend it as I like?" she asked, anxiously.

"Certainly," returned Mrs. Tyrell, and then very irrelevantly—the little girl considered—she began to speak of Widow Cronin's honesty, and of her poverty; of Maggie's disappointment when she found that the money did not belong to her, and her desire to do right at any cost; of how children who were poorly clad must suffer from cold in winter.

Pollie did not pay much attention. It was not a pleasing picture which her mother drew. Still, she could not help thinking of it afterward: and, oddly enough, she changed her mind about going that very afternoon to Brown's great store to select her gifts from the new stock of elegant knick-knacks and toys. "After all," said she, "there is no need of being in a hurry. I'll wait and find out what everyone would like best."

A day or two passed, but Pollie was more undecided than at first. She made innumerable lists, and, as soon as completed, tore them up again; she calculated the cost of a variety of articles, but in turn rejected the idea of getting any of them; for when she was sure she had fixed upon something, and had set the price down on a piece of paper, opposite the figures, she seemed to see as plainly as if it were really written there: "Just the price of a pair of shoes!" "How many pairs of stockings would that buy?" "Poor girls like pretty things too!" And presently, in desperation, she would begin all over again.

One night, Pollie had a curious dream. She thought she saw first one pair of little bare feet come skipping up before her; then ten, twenty, fifty, went stumbling past—nothing but feet. All looked blue and cold, while some were so tiny and toddling that she longed to warm them with her hands and wrap them in the folds of her woollen dress. It was a pitiable spectacle, and Pollie shivered as she saw them scurrying along over the ice and snow. While she was pondering how queer it was, and wishing she could follow them, lo and behold! they all came dancing, prancing, capering back, clad in scarlet stockings and shiny boots, and led by—Pollie thought she should die laughing—the brightest of little red feathers, which marshalled all the twinkling, frolicsome company with the air of a general. And then, at the word of command, they all vanished.

The next morning, Pollie laughed every time the recollection of the dream occurred to her. Nevertheless, it became harder than ever to decide upon her gifts. Wherever she went a pair of wee bare feet seemed to pop up in front of her; an aggressive red feather looked out from every corner. She was haunted by the memory of the needy Cronin children. But to Pollie, with her inclination to vanity, it was Maggie's pathetic, childish longing for a bit of finery which appealed with especial force.

That afternoon, she encountered the little girl coming to the house to ask if Mrs. Tyrell had any work for her mother.

"Maggie," said Pollie on the spur of the moment, "do you remember all you were going to do with the money you found in the brown dress?"

"Yes, indeed," replied the latter, her face lighting up at the remembrance, though the next moment she sighed to think how idle her scheme had been.

"Would you like really to have those things to give to your mother and the children?" asked Pollie, breathing hard, and making up her mind in a trice.

"Oh!" cried Maggie, quite overpowered.

"Well, I've been thinking," Pollie went on, dashing boldly into the subject, "that if you had not brought back that five dollar bill I should not have it at all, and that the best way to spend it would be for us to go down to Brown's together for those very things."

"Oh!" stammered Maggie again, wondering if she was actually awake; for this seemed too remarkable to come to pass.

"We cannot buy them all," continued Pollie, regretfully: "but I shall only keep enough of the money to get a small 'angel lamp,' for the Blessed Virgin's altar in the Claytonville church, because I had nothing to offer on Our Lady's birthday. Wait, and we'll go in a minute."

Pollie rushed into the house, spoke a word to Mamma, took the five dollars out of her work-box, and, before Maggie could realize what was happening, they were on their way to Brown's.

As they reached the store, who should they meet but Mr. Brown himself? Pollie knew him well, for he was an intimate friend of Mr. Tyrell's, and often visited the family. When he saw the little girls, he stopped, and said, cheerily:

"Good afternoon, Miss Pollie. What can we do for you today?"

Pollie answered blithely, and then, she felt so happy that she found herself telling him the whole story of the five dollars. Mr. Brown appeared very much interested. When she had finished, he told one of the clerks to make every effort to suit his young friends. Thus their shopping progressed finely.

But when Pollie had purchased her "angel lamp"— which she got at a bargain—and Maggie had bought shoes and stockings for Biddeen, and Jim, and Patsy, they found to their dismay that they had only twenty-five cents left.

"Well, there's enough to get the red wing, anyhow!" said Pollie, gladly.

"Oh, no!" cried Maggie; "we haven't anything for Mother yet!"

So, with a pang she relinquished all hope of the feather, and they decided upon a pair of warm gloves for Mrs. Cronin.

While they were waiting for their parcels, another clerk came along in great haste, carrying a big, comfortable-looking shawl.

"Mr. Brown," said he, "sends this to little Maggie Cronin for her mother. And he wishes her to pick out the brightest, prettiest red feather for herself."

The girls were overjoyed. Maggie did not take long to make her choice, and then, they returned to the Tyrells', where another delightful surprise awaited them. Mrs. Tyrell had found a suit of half-worn clothes belonging to John, which she gave to Maggie for Patsy; and Papa, who seemed to know all that was going on, said, patting Pollie on the head with a look of proud satisfaction, and smiling kindly at Maggie: "I'll see about the coal and the blankets, children." Maggie was sent home, laden with packages, and feeling that she was the happiest little girl in the whole world.

Gertrude, who had spent the day with her friends, the Mortons, knew nothing of the various episodes of the afternoon. Neither did the boys; nor, of course, baby Toosie. In the evening, the mischief-loving brothers were in a particularly teasing humor.

"Hie Pollie! Aren't you ever going to spend your five dollars?" asked John, when he could not think of anything else to annoy her about.

"Ho, little miser! Where do you hide your money-bags?" cried Rob, mockingly.

Pollie, after the pleasurable excitement of the last few hours, was a trifle nervous and tearful. At last, breaking away from her tormentors, she rushed upstairs, and locked herself in her own room.

"Little miser! little miser!" cried the boys.

"Children," remonstrated Mrs. Tyrell, "beware of rash judgments! What right have you to call Pollie a miser? Listen! I have a story for you." She astonished them by telling how the five-dollar note was lost and found, and of the use Pollie had made of it.

Before the end, Gertrude slipped away, and induced her sister to come down to the sitting-room again. As they reached the door, Pollie, to her amazement, was greeted with a perfect ovation.

"Hurrah for Pollie!" cheered the boys, baby Toosie chiming in with her sweet treble; while Papa clapped his hands, and Mamma laughed merrily. "Hurrah for Pollie! Hurrah for Pollie's five dollars!"

No!

"A, c-o-n con, Acon, c-a ca, Aconca— Oh, dear, what a hard word! Let me see— A-con-ca-gua. I never can pronounce it, I am sure. I wish they would not have such hard names in geography," said George Gould, quite out of patience. "Will you please tell me how to pronounce the name of this mountain, Father?"

"Why do you call that a hard word, George? I know much harder ones than that."

"Well, Father, this is the hardest word I ever saw," replied George. "I wish they had put the name into the volcano, and burnt it up."

"I know how to pronounce it," said Jane. "It is A-conca—gua!"

"A-con-ca—gua," said George, stopping at each syllable. "Well, it is not so very hard after all; but I wish they would not have any long words, and then I could pronounce them easily enough."

"I do not think so," said his father. "Some of the hardest words I have ever seen are the shortest. I know one little word, with only two letters in it, that very few children, or men either, can always speak."

"Oh, I suppose it is some French or German word; isn't it, Father?"

"No, it is English; and you may think it strange, but it is just as hard to pronounce in one language as another."

"Only two letters! What can it be?" cried both the children.

"The hardest word," continued Father, "I have ever met with in any language — and I have learned several — is the little word of two letters— N-o, No."

"Now you are making fun of us!" cried the children; "that is one of the easiest words in the world." And to prove that their father was mistaken, they both repeated, "No, no, no," a great many times.

"I am not joking in the least," said their father. "I really think it is the hardest of all words. It may seem easy enough to you tonight, but perhaps you can not pronounce it tomorrow."

"I can always say it; I know I can," said George, with much confidence. "No! Why, it is as easy to say it as to breathe."

"Well, George, I hope you will always find it as easy to pronounce as you think it is now, and be able to speak it when you ought to."

In the morning, George went bravely to school, a little proud that he could pronounce so hard a word as "Aconcagua." Not far from the schoolhouse was a large pond of very deep water, where the boys used to skate and slide when it was frozen over.

Now, the night before, Jack Frost had been busy changing the surface of the pond into hard, clear ice, which the boys in the morning found as smooth as glass. The day was cold, and they thought that by noon the ice would be strong enough to bear their weight.

As soon as the school was out, the boys all ran to

the pond, some to try the ice, and others merely to
see it.

"Come, George," said William Green, "now we
will have a glorious time sliding." George hesitated,
and said he did not believe it was strong enough, for
it had been frozen over only one night.

"Oh, come on!" said another boy; "I know it is
strong enough. I have known it to freeze over in
one night, many a time, so it would bear my weight.
Haven't you, John?"

"Yes," answered John Brown, "it did one night last
winter, and it wasn't so cold as it was last night, either."

But George still hesitated, for his father had forbidden him to go on the ice without special permission.

"I know why George won't go," said John; "he's
afraid he might fall and hurt himself."

"Or the ice might crack," said another. "Perhaps
his mother might not like it."

"He's a coward; that's the reason he won't come."

George could stand this no longer, for he was rather proud of his courage. "I am not afraid" said he; and he ran to the pond and was the first one on the ice. The boys enjoyed the sport very much, running and sliding, and trying to catch one another.

More boys kept coming on as they saw the sport, and all began to think there was no danger, when suddenly there was a loud cry, "The ice has broken! the ice has broken!" And sure enough, three of the boys had broken through and were struggling in the water. One of them was George.

The teacher had been attracted by the noise, and was coming to call the boys from the ice just as they broke through. He tore off some boards from a fence close by, and shoved them out on the ice until they came within reach of the boys in the water. After a while he succeeded in getting them out, but not until they were nearly frozen.

George's father and mother were very much frightened when he was brought home, and they learned how narrowly he had escaped drowning. But they were so rejoiced to find that he was safe, that they did not ask him how he came to go on the ice, until after tea. When they were all gathered together about the cheerful fire, his father asked him how he came to disobey his positive command. George said that he did not want to go, but the boys made him.

"How did they make you? Did they take hold of you and drag you on?" asked his father.

"No," said George; "but they all wanted me to go."

"When they asked you, why didn't you say 'No'?"

"I was going to; but they called me a coward, and

said I was afraid to go, and I couldn't stand that."

"And so," said his father, "you found it easier to disobey me, and run the risk of losing your life, than to say that little word you thought so easy last night. You could not say 'No'!"

George now began to see why this little word "No" was so hard to pronounce. It was not because it was so long, or composed of such difficult sounds; but because it often requires so much real courage to say it — to say "No" when one is tempted to do wrong.

Whenever, in after-life, George was tempted to do wrong, he remembered his narrow escape, and the importance of the little word "No." The more often he said it, the easier it became; and in time he could say it, when needed, without much effort.

Mary's Sacrifice

There were four children in the Beresford family: Dermot, Brian, Mary and Kathleen. The children looked upon their parents as the best and greatest people in the world. It is not necessary to describe the character of the young Beresfords. They had some of the faults and some of the virtues usually ascribed to American children. Mary was just fifteen years of age; Brian and Dermot were twins and one year younger than Mary, and Kathleen was twelve.

Mr. Beresford sat at the breakfast table on a certain morning in spring, and looked at the bright faces on either side of him. Mr. Beresford's hair had begun to turn gray lately. Mary, so lovingly observant, noticed that the wrinkles near his eyes made a network of fine lines. He said grace and then said, "I have news for you, children."

"Good news?" asked the twins.

"I don't know," said Mr. Beresford. "I cannot say what you children will think of it."

"You have found a school for us!" cried Dermot, looking up excitedly. "I knew we would get to go some day."

Mrs. Beresford smiled sadly. "Ah, dear boys," she said, "would you be gloomy if you were told that father could not afford to send you to college at all; and that you must begin to work for your living?"

Mrs. Beresford's blue eyes filled with tears, and her voice trembled a little.

Brian and Dermot dropped their spoons in surprise.

"Yes, boys," said Mr. Beresford, "your mother has hinted at the truth. My business ventures in the West have gone wrong. The Stalacta Mines, in which all my earnings were invested, is a failure. And Doctor Jarvis says that I shall die, unless I get into the country as soon as possible. When I sell this house I may have enough money to buy a farm. I hoped, as you know, to send you to a good school for several years; but I cannot do it now. Well, well—how do you like the idea of farming?"

Dermot said nothing. He hung his head, and if he had been a younger boy, a tear would have dropped into his oatmeal. It was a great disappointment.

Brian, on the contrary, was much relieved. He often said to himself that it was a shame for his father to be growing gray-haired over old law books in an office, while Dermot and he studied or played. His own white hands filled him with disgust. He said he wanted to work.

Mary's eyes brightened. "And I can really help mother! Oh, I think farming will be nice!"

Mrs. Beresford shook her head. "We shall be very poor."

"Why, Mother," said Mary, "haven't you told us often that if we were contented and good, poverty made no difference? We shall all be together. Isn't that enough?"

"It is a great sacrifice for you all to leave this fine house and the lively city," said Mr. Beresford, "but I must ask it of you. It is my duty to save my life and health until you are able to take care of yourselves. I know you will all help me."

Dermot went to his father and put his arms around his neck. "Dear Father," he said, with tears in his eyes, "I will do anything for your sake."

"Come, let's be cheerful and talk over our plans."

Mary went upstairs after breakfast. She drew from a wardrobe a pretty white gown. It was soft and, here and there among its folds, rested brilliant silver lace. She looked at it sadly. It had been given to her on her birthday. She had not yet worn it, and her father had promised to let her invite as many of her friends as she chose, in honor of his birthday, which would be late in May. But now that was all over. She could not remind her father of his promise.

The sunlight on the pretty gown made the silver lace glisten like the reflections of light on a rippling stream. Mary sighed.

Alice Howe had given a party; Agnes Richards had given a luncheon to all her young friends, and Mildred Ellis had had a delightful *musicale*, with singing by all her class in school, and a man to play the zither. The girls would think it strange if she did not give them a little fun before she went into the country. The tears came into her eyes. She felt tempted to ask her father; he would understand and let her have a celebration on his birthday. She knew he would! But then he was so worried about other things. And then the expense! She heard his step sounding in his study. She would just run in and ask him. It would be so nice to wear that pretty dress. She made a movement towards the door.

Was she selfish, she asked herself? She looked at the Madonna and the Child that stood on the pedestal in one corner of her room. Sister Hortense and her dear mother had often told her that in times of difficulty, she ought to say a Hail Mary, and to try to model her conduct on that of the Blessed Virgin. She thought of her father's bowed head and the wrinkles around his eyes. She said her Hail Mary. Then, with a sigh, she put the soft gown back into its box and cried a little.

She had just wiped her eyes when a flutter was heard on the stairs. She opened the door and a girl about her own age came in and hugged her hard. It was Alice Howe. Alice moved with as much vivacity as she could, considering that her dress was very tight, and that she had a little dog which she led by a string. She threw herself into a chair, while the dog sniffed around the room.

"Oh, dear!" she said, in an affected imitation of what she thought to be an English tone of voice, "I'm quite too awfully tired. You really ought to have an elevator in this big house. I've just run in to ask you to my luncheon, on the 28th. It will be quite lovely. Mamma has ordered favors for twenty girls, and Papa has promised me that the flowers shall be something *superb*. You must come, and wear your new dress."

Alice, a pleasant looking girl, with wide open blue eyes and yellow hair, was, unfortunately, spoiled by affectation. She had all the airs and graces of a veteran woman of society. Her parents were too busy with other and less important matters to give her much attention.

Mary's manner was very simple and childish, compared with the airs of Alice; but Mary could look one directly in the face, with a clear and honest gaze.

"You are very kind, Alice," Mary answered, "but I think we will be out of town by the 28th."

"So soon! When are you going? It's just the time for Atlantic City, before the crush begins—"

"No, no," said Mary, hastily, "we are not going away for pleasure. Poor Father is not well, and we are going into the country to live."

"Not for good!" cried Alice.

"Yes."

"You can't mean it. What, are you to give up the riding club, and the party you promised us? You certainly are crazy, Mary."

"The truth is," said Mary, with an effort and a slight blush, "we're too poor to live here."

Alice leaned back in her chair and laughed.

"This is quite too awfully funny! Fancy"—she said 'fawncy'—"living in a house like this, with Mexican onyx mantel pieces, and real lace curtains, and talking that way! Papa often does the same thing, whenever I want him to buy me anything pretty. But Mamma and I don't mind it! Poof! The idea! It's just your papa's talk!"

"No," said Mary, gravely, "Father always means what he says. We shall all have to work hard on a farm somewhere."

"What!" cried Alice, "*you don't* mean it! Oh, this is quite too dreadfully, awfully horrible, *you* churn the butter and milk the cows, feed the pigs and gather potatoes! Oh, my dear, your father can't be so awfully cruel! And you'll have no chance of wearing your new dress on a farm! Come now, you do not mean it?"

"Father said, this very morning, we must go away and live very carefully," Mary answered, with an effort. "I suppose if one is poor, one may be good and contented, and nice, if one tries."

"Impossible!" Alice said, running her fingers through her bangs, to show a diamond ring she wore. "Poor people never can be nice. Just to think of living in a little house, with no servants, and having always to ride in a streetcar. Poor people are always nasty."

"Our Lord was poor. Sister Hortense told us, over and over again, to remember that. And the Blessed Virgin was poor."

Alice was silent for an instant. "Oh, that was a long time ago. Don't preach, Mary, please. Just think of it, this morning, almost before I was up, Mother came and asked me if I had a white dress I didn't want. I was quite paralyzed by the question, for Mamma knows very well that I want everything I have. It seems that a poor woman, who lives behind our house, had the impudence to ask Mamma for a dress, so that her daughter could make her First

Holy Communion dressed in white, like the other girls. To be fair, she only wanted to borrow one, and having heard that I went to the convent school, she thought Mamma might lend her one of mine! Fancy! She said it would be a great favor, as she could not afford to buy a white dress. Did you ever hear of such a thing? I was very angry!"

Mary was silent. A slight color came to her face.

"You aggravating girl," continued Alice, "you won't give me a bit of sympathy. Imagine your laundry woman asking you for a gown. I guess you'd be very angry, too."

"No," said Mary, "I would not."

"What virtue!" cried Alice sarcastically. "I should like to see you lend her one of your white dresses, the new one, for instance!"

Mary walked over to the bookcase and l o o k e d at the pretty rows of gilded books. Alice's words had struck home.

"The girl's name is Anna Doran and she lives in Wilbert's Court. There, my dear friend! Don't preach to me unless you practice what you preach. To

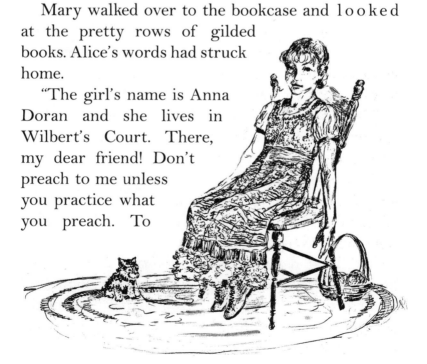

change the subject, I shall have my new fan painted for your party."

"Alice, believe me, there will be no more parties for me. We are poor now, and we shall all have to work."

Alice went close to Mary and looked into her face. "Are you really in earnest?"

"Indeed I am!"

"Bosh!" cried Alice, "Come live with me. You can have half my room. Let the boys be poor if they want to. You come and live with us."

Mary laughed. "Oh, Alice, how silly you are! How could I leave Father, Mother, and Kathleen? I must help them. I shall study hard, if I have to stay up all night. I know Sister Hortense will give me a list of books. I will practice a great deal, too."

"Poor people don't have pianos."

"Perhaps Father may let me keep mine."

Alice threw herself back in her chair and laughed. She mimicked Mary's last sentence, over and over again, with much apparent enjoyment.

"Oh, dear," she cried at last, "you will kill me! Perhaps your papa will buy you a monkey, and then you can go about the streets like an Italian and help to support the family."

Alice saw a dangerous sparkle in Mary's eye, for Mary had by nature what is called a "temper," but she had been taught to control it.

"Well, good-bye, Mary. If you will take summer boarders when you go on the farm, I'll come. But I think it's real mean about your party. And all the girls will talk it over and say unkind things. It will be quite too awfully foolish!"

Alice kissed Mary on both cheeks and then bounded away.

Left alone, Mary knelt down near the wide window seat and cried. All the girls who had often entertained Mary would say she was too mean to keep her promise about the birthday party. They would talk about it in school. Sister Hortense would give her comfort, she knew; but then, Sister Hortense was not one of the girls, and she could not control their thoughts and speech. It did look mean, Mary admitted to herself. She had talked so much about the party and her new gown.

She opened the box that enclosed the precious article. She said to herself that she would wear it; she would speak to her father and tell him that he ought to give her a last party. How lovely the dress would look, if she could only wear it and have one more good time, in spite of everything.

Somehow or other, just then, she calmed. It would not be serving God to worry her dear father just now, and perhaps, coax him into spending money for luxuries that he really needed for necessities.

If she could only wear that lovely white dress, just once! But no, she was a poor girl now.

Alice Howe's visit had disturbed her. It had made her uneasy and discontented. The incident of the child whose mother wanted to borrow the white dress came into her mind. Ought she to make a sacrifice and give up this beautiful gown?

She ran down to the sitting room to find her mother. She was busy at her small desk attending to her correspondence.

"Yes, Mary?" she said.

"Mother, Alice Howe has just been telling me of a poor girl who has no dress to wear at her First Holy Communion, and I thought"—Mrs. Beresford looked a little troubled. "You know, my dear, we are not as we used to be, and I am afraid I have no white fabric that would do for such a dress. And I don't think you have any that would suit."

"Oh, yes, I have," said Mary, eagerly. "My new one!"

Mrs. Beresford smiled. "Where do these people live—the people Alice spoke of?"

"Back in the court. Their name is Doran."

Mrs. Beresford's face brightened. "Oh yes, a very respectable family. The father is a chronic invalid, in a hospital. The mother did some work for me when Delia was sick. You can go over. I think, though, that if you give the young girl your dress, you had better remove the silver lace. It would look conspicuous and out of place."

"Very well, Mother. Can I go now?"

Mrs. Beresford smiled, and Mary ran off to get her hat.

It was only a few days until the great feast when the children of the parish were to make their First Holy Communion. There was preparation in many households. The boys would wear new suits, if possible, with white rosettes on their lapels and the girls were to have white dresses with blue sashes.

Anna Doran had passed her examination for that happy group that was to approach the altar. Anna was thirteen years old and large for her age, in fact, she was quite as stout and a little taller than Mary Beresford. She had lived in the country, far from a church, and her First Holy Communion had been postponed when she was younger.

The Dorans were very poor. Dick, Anna's elder brother, lay on a lounge in their little parlor, unable to move. He had been thrown from a wagon and internally injured. Mrs. Doran went to people's homes to wash and iron their laundry. Anna was obliged to stay at home, to nurse Dick.

These days Anna was unusually silent. Generally, she was very happy and cheerful, but today her fits of quietness made her brother wonder.

Anna had a deep grief in her heart. She had only two worn and patched dresses. They might be made to do in the street, for they were always neat and clean, but they were so old and rust colored from hard wear, that she could not wear either of them in church on the great day. Oh, if she only had a white dress! It was useless to wish for such an impossible thing. Her mother could scarcely get sufficient money to pay the rent and Dick's medicine bill.

Dick would have given her a dress, if he were well and able to earn money. And her dear father could not do it either. They had never let father know how poor they were. He was looking forward to seeing Anna come to his bedside at the hospital, in her white dress, after the function at the church. Tears came into Anna's eyes when she thought of his disappointment.

Her mother had thought of asking Mrs. Howe for an old dress of Alice's. We know how that turned out. The time was so near, and nobody would help her to do the thing she most wanted—though it was a little thing! She saw many girls in the street carelessly wearing white dresses, and she had to say a Hail Mary to save herself from envying them. While Dick slept, she had tenderly washed his face and hands and combed his hair. Then Anna took out her rosary and prayed that she might be allowed to make her First Holy Communion with the others.

"After all," she thought, "Our dear Lord will know best." And then the fear and anxiety left her. She busied herself with arranging a few flowers, which were sent to Dick by a neighboring market woman. There was a knock on the door. Anna opened the door, and Mary stood on the threshold, smiling a little.

"May I come in?"

"Certainly," answered Anna, recognizing her guest, for she had seen her at church, "you are Miss Beresford, are you not?"

"I am Mary Beresford." And, catching sight of the covered figure on the sofa asked, "Is your brother sick?"

"Yes," said Anna, "he is better now, he's asleep."

Anna gave her a chair, and as she noticed how neat and tasteful her guest's dress was, she wished her dress were less shabby. Then the remembrance of her own trouble, concerning a dress, came to her and she sighed.

Mary's quick ear caught the sigh. "I must tell you why I came; I hope you will not be offended. I was told that you were to make your First Holy Communion with the others in a few days."

"Not with the others, I'm afraid."

An eager question rose to Mary's lips, but she did not speak it. She waited for Anna to go on, but Anna

Rare Catholic Stories

paused. Mary felt it difficult to mention the dress, now that she had come.

Suddenly, Dick, who had been dozing and was not aware that a stranger was present, spoke, "If I were rich, Anna, do you know what I'd do? Why, I'd just buy you a new dress, so that you could look like the other girls."

"Hush Dick, Miss Beresford is here."

Dick looked up and smiled at Mary. He was very pale; but his half-open eyes, his red hair, and even his weak voice expressed good nature. Dick nodded towards Mary and then relapsed into sleep.

"I came to ask you if I might give you a dress I have," said Mary, plunging into the subject in desperation, "I haven't worn it, and if you would please take it, I would be obliged."

Anna could scarcely take in the words.

"It is a nice white dress, and I think it will fit you."

Anna hid her face in her hands, and Mary saw tears trickling through her fingers.

"I am so sorry—I hope you are not offended...."

"Offended!" cried Anna, taking away her hands and looking at Mary with tear-filled eyes. "You don't know how happy you have made me! It seemed so dreadful not to be able to go with the others. And Father would be so disappointed if I did not go in white. Oh, dear, if you will only lend me your dress, I shall be very, very happy!"

Mary's face glowed with pleasure. "I want to give it to you, if you will take it. You are just about my size. I'll send it over this afternoon. I must go now. Good-bye!"

Mary hurried away to escape Anna's thanks. All her forebodings were forgotten—all her desire to wear her pretty dress was gone—she almost ran home. She met Alice Howe coming out of a confectioner's shop, with a big box of chocolate *bon-bons*. Alice called to her, but Mary shook her head, as she was eager to get home.

It didn't take her long to rip the silver lace off of the white gown. She did it, singing cheerfully. She knew now how sweet it is to make others happy. Her mother gave her some thin fabric for a veil for Anna, and some blue ribbon. In the afternoon, Mary put the precious dress in its box, and, with the veil and ribbon wrapped in tissue paper, went with Kathleen to Wilbert's Court.

Kathleen talked quite happily to Dick while Anna tried on the dress, and Mary critically inspected it in the kitchen. A little pinning and a few stitches made the dress just right.

Anna forgot her bashfulness in the excitement of the process, and Mary had so many suggestions to make, that she talked a lot and very fast—an unusual thing with her. At last Anna stood arrayed in the new dress. Dick almost jumped from his sofa in delight.

Smiling and blushing, Anna let them admire. While they were still admiring, Mrs. Doran entered, tired and worn out, laden with brooms, brushes and a bucket. She understood the situation at a glance.

She sat down on a chair near the door and looked at Anna. Then she looked at Mary and tried to speak. "God bless you, my dear," she tried to say and her voice choked. She began to sob. "You don't know what a kindness you've done."

When Mrs. Doran had wiped her eyes, she asked Mary to have tea with the family. Mary said she would, partly because she feared to offend Mrs. Doran, and partly because she wanted to see how poor people live. She expected to be very poor herself, and she would like to know how the poor lived.

Anna was not long in getting tea ready. A round table was moved over near Dick's sofa, so that he could sit up and have his tea, too. A teapot and five cups and saucers were produced and put on the white cloth, with some bread and raspberry jam. Mary, who expected to see tin cups and perhaps wooden spoons, was pleasantly surprised. Everything was as clean and as shining as at home. Kathleen laughed and chatted away, and enjoyed her tea very much. After a pleasant hour, Mary and Kathleen said good-bye.

In the evening, Mary told her father all about her visit. He was very much interested. "And so you gave away your new dress?"

"It wasn't much loss to me, Father, I didn't need it."

"Well, my dear," said her father, smiling—how that smile on his pale face cheered her in years to come—"I've heard the Carmelite Nuns say, 'May God reward you,' when they hear of a good deed. I say with all my heart now: May God reward you, my child!"

The Blacksmith of Ragenbach

One afternoon in early autumn, a party of men and women were chatting and laughing in the tavern room of Ragenbach, a little village in Germany. The village blacksmith was one of the merry company. He was a good-natured man, with a kind, honest face, and greatly liked by his neighbors. His arms were like bars of iron, his hands large and powerful, and he was as noted for his strength as for his good temper.

He sat near the entrance talking with a neighbor, when all at once the door swung back, and a large, powerful dog staggered into the room. Its head hung down, its eyes were bloodshot; its breast was flecked with foam, and its lead-colored tongue lolled halfway out its mouth.

No sooner had the blacksmith's neighbor set eyes on the beast than he turned deadly pale, and exclaimed, "Holy Mother, save us! The dog is mad!" The little room was full, and the only means of egress was the door before which the rabid animal now stood. It snapped, savagely, right and left, and to attempt to pass it meant a sure and terrible death.

Horror was stamped on every face. Strong men thought of their wives; mothers of their children! Who was to deliver them from this danger? Amid all this tumult, the blacksmith alone stood still and

Rare Catholic Stories

fearless. He saw the anguish of the people; and as he thought how many families could be made desolate in a few minutes, he resolved to save them if he could.

Stepping forward, he said in his deep, strong voice, as quietly as if death did not stare him in the face, "Back, every one of you. Someone must die to save the others. Let me be that one. I alone can hold that beast. Let no one move until I seize it. Then, while I have it securely in my grasp, let every one leave the room."

Scarcely had he finished speaking when the rabid animal rushed at the terrified, shrieking people. But it did not go far. "With the help of God!" cried the

blacksmith, and he threw himself on the foaming beast, seized it in his iron grasp, and dashed it to the floor.

A terrible struggle followed. The dog bit furiously on every side. Its long teeth tore the arms and thighs of the heroic man, who never for an instant relaxed his hold. Regardless alike of the pain and horrible death that was sure to ensue, he held the snapping, howling brute until everyone had escaped. He then flung the half-strangled beast from him, dashing it against the wall, and left the room, locking the door after him. A shot through the window disposed of the dog.

The grateful people flocked around their preserver, thanking him for his noble, generous deed, while weeping at the thought that he had saved their lives only at the sacrifice of his own. "Grieve not for me," he said. "I have only done my duty. All I ask is that when I am dead, you will think of me with love; and now pray for me, that our dear Lord will not let me suffer long nor too much. I will take care that no harm comes to you through me."

Going to his workshop, he selected the best and heaviest chain he could find, and with his own hands welded it firmly around his body and then to a weighty anvil. "There," said he, "it is done. Now I can do no harm. As long as I live, bring me food. The rest I leave to God. Into His hands I commend my spirit."

After suffering some days, death came to the blacksmith's relief. He died, but his memory lives in the small village from generation to generation.

Apples, Ripe and Rosy, Sir

The temperature was sharp and frosty, the ground white, the clouds heavy with snow. The storm of the night before had only ceased temporarily; it would begin again soon—a few flakes were already floating in the air. By early afternoon the children began to troop out of their homes. How pleasant to watch the throng of bright-eyed, chattering little girls, in coats and hoods and mittens, and a crowd of sturdy boys trudging along discussing games and sports, and others indulging in a little random snowballing of their comrades. Half an hour later the snow was falling thick and fast. A number of boys had gathered in one of the parks and were busy completing a snowfort. People hurried home; it was sure to be a disagreeable evening.

These indications were sadly noted by one person in particular, to whom they meant more than to others in general. This was the good, old Irishwoman who kept the apple and peanut stand at the street corner, and who was the center of attraction to the children.

"Wisha, this is goin' to be a cold night, I'm thinkin'!" sighed she, wrapping a faded and much-worn shawl more securely about her, and striving to protect both herself and her wares beneath the shelter of an old umbrella. "What bad luck I've had today!" she continued under her breath, still scanning the faces of the passersby, though she now had little hope that any would pause to buy. "An' it's a bigger lot than usual I laid in, too. The peanuts is extry size; an' them apples look so fine and rosy, I thought it 'ud make anybody's mouth water to see them. I counted upon the boys to buy them up in a twinklin', by reason of me markin' them down to two for a cent. An' so they would, but they're so taken up with sportin' in the snow that they can think of nothin' else. An' now that it's turned so raw, sure I'm afraid it's cold comfort any one but a lad would think it, settin' his teeth on edge tryin' to eat them. I'll tarry a bit longer; an' then I'll take meself to me little room, even though I'll have to drink me tea without a tint of milk or a dust of sugar tonight."

Patiently she waited. The clock struck five. As no other customers appeared, the old woman, who was known as Widow Barry, concluded that she would be movin' on home.

The stand consisted of a large basket, a campseat, and the umbrella, which was intended to afford, not only a roof, but an air of dignity to the stand, and was therefore always open, rain or shine.

To "shut up shop," though it meant simply to lower the umbrella, gather up the goods and depart, was to the apple vender a momentous affair. The widow was obliged literally to carry her establishment. To make her way, thus laden, in the midst of a driving snowstorm was indeed a difficult matter. Half a dozen times she faltered in discouragement. The street led over a steep hill; how was she to reach the top? She struggled along; the wind blew through her thin garments; the umbrella bobbed wildly about; her hands grew numb; the basket kept slipping from her grasp. Several persons passed, but no one seemed to think of stopping to assist her. A group of boys were sledding down the middle of the street; what did they care about the storm? Several boys, who were standing awaiting their turn, glanced idly at the poor woman.

With a laugh, Ed Brown sent a well-aimed snowball straight against the umbrella, which shook with a thud. Then the group whizzed by, without another thought of the aged creature toiling up the hill. No one appeared to have time to help her.

Presently, however, she heard a firm, light step behind her. The next moment a pair of merry brown eyes peered under the umbrella; a face beamed upon her with the smile of old friendship, and a happy, young voice cried out:

"Good afternoon, Mrs. Barry! It's hard work getting on today, isn't it?"

A gentle expression lighted up the apple-woman's weather-beaten face as she recognized the little fellow, who was evidently returning from an errand, as he carried a milk can in one hand while drawing a sled with the other.

"Indade an' it is, Tom!" she replied, pausing a second.

"Let us see if we can't manage differently," he went on, taking her burden and setting it upon the sled. "There, that is better."

"Oh, thank ye kindly! It's too much for ye to be takin' this trouble."

"No trouble at all," said he. "Follow me, I'll pick

out the best places for you to walk in—the snow is drifting so!"

He trudged on ahead, glancing back occasionally to see if the basket and campseat were safe, or to direct her steps—as if all this were the most natural thing in the world for him to do, as in truth it was. He and Widow Barry had been good friends for some time. Tom, moreover, was a regular patron of "the stand."

"Sure, an' didn't he buy out me whole supply one day this last January?" she would say. "His birthday it was, and the dear boy was eleven years old. He spent the big silver dollar his grandfather gave him, a treatin' all the boys of the neighborhood to apples an' peanuts, an' sendin' me home to rest."

Upon reaching the Widow Barry's home, Tom scampered off with an especially good-looking apple, which the woman forced into his hand.

"Ah, but he's the dear, generous-hearted boy!" she exclaimed, as she stood looking after him. "There's not a bit of worldly pride or meanness about him. May the Lord keep him so! The only thing I'd be afraid of is that he'll be easily led. There's that Ed Brown now—Heaven forgive me, but somehow I don't like that lad. Though he's the son of the richest man in the neighborhood, he's no fit companion for Tom Norris, I'm thinkin'."

* * * *

As Widow Barry had thought, Tom was easily led, and therein rested the possibilities of great good or evil. As he mingled more with other boys, he was not always steadfast in acting up to his knowledge of what was right, and he was apt to be influenced by his companions. At present he was making a chum of Ed Brown, who, though only a year older, was shrewd and what the world calls "smart."

The old woman had, indeed, many opportunities for observation; for is not sometimes so simple an action as buying an apple a real test of character? If a boy or girl is tricky or mean or unjust in little things, is it likely that we shall find him or her upright and honorable in larger things? Tom's mother had positively forbade Tom to have any more to do with Ed—a command which he grumbled a good deal about, and, alas, occasionally disobeyed.

But to continue our story. On the following Saturday morning, the skies were blue, the sun shone bright, the gladness of spring was in the air. The apple stand at the corner had a prosperous aspect. The umbrella, though shabbier than ever, had a cheery look. Widow Barry was engaged in polishing up her apples and arranging the peanuts as invitingly as possible; a number of pennies already jingled in the small bag attached to her apron string, in which she kept her money.

"Ah, here comes Tom!" she exclaimed, presently.

"Hello, Mrs. Barry!" cried he. "How's business today? Too early to tell yet? Well, see if I can't help it a little. Give me a dozen apples, and one—yes, two bags of nuts."

Pleased and flustered at this stroke of fortune, she busied herself in getting out two of the largest of her paper bags and filling the large order. But Tom was not like himself this morning. He had plenty to say; but he talked quickly with a kind of forced happiness, and he was eager to be off.

The old woman paused a second, as if suddenly impressed by the difference in his manner. With a pleasant word she put the well-filled bags into Tom's hands and received the money he offered in payment—three bright new dimes. At that moment she caught a glimpse of Ed Brown lurking by a house at the other end of the block. The sight filled her with a vague misgiving. She glanced at Tom.

"Wait a bit," she said, laying a hand upon his arm.

"What is the matter? Didn't I give you the right amount?" he asked impatiently.

The old woman bent forward and peered anxiously into his face; her kind but searching eyes seemed to look down into his very soul, as, in a voice trembling with emotion, she replied: "Yes. But tell me, where did ye get the money?"

Tom's countenance changed; he tried to put her off, saying, "Pshaw! Why do you want to ask a fellow such a question? Haven't I bought more than this from you before?"

"Ye have, dear; but not in this way, I'm thinkin'," she answered.

"It's all right. Do let me go, Mrs. Barry!" cried he, beginning to feel decidedly frightened.

"Hi, Tom, come on!" called Ed Brown, emerging from around the corner of the house.

"Look here, Tom, darlin'! You'll not move a step with them things, until I know where the money came from."

"Well, then," said Tom, doggedly, seeing that escape was impossible, "I got it at home, off the mantel in the sitting room."

"Oh, no!" ejaculated Mrs. Barry, raising her eyes toward Heaven, as if praying for the pardon of the offence.

"Why, that's nothing!" he went on. "Ed Brown says lots of boys do it. Some take the change out of their father's pockets even, if they get a chance. His father doesn't mind a bit. He always has plenty of cash, Ed has."

"Ah, yes, that ne'er-do-well, Ed Brown!" said the old woman, shaking her fist at the distant Ed, who, realizing that Tom had got into trouble, disappeared in a twinkling.

"An' his father don't mind! Then it's because he knows nothin' about it. They'll come a day of reckonin' for him. An' you—"

"Oh, my parents won't care!" persisted Tom, thoroughly ashamed, but still anxious to excuse himself. "Mother always says that everything in the house is for the use of the family. If we children should make a raid on the pantry, and carry off a pie or cake, she might punish us for the disobedience, but she wouldn't call it stealing." He blushed as he uttered the ugly word.

"Yes, but to take money is different, ye know," continued his relentless mentor, whose heart was sorrowing over him with the tenderness of a mother for her child.

Tom was silent; he did know, had really known from the first, though now his fault stood before him in its ugliness; all the excuses with which he had attempted to hide it fell from it like a veil, showing the hateful thing it was. He could not bring himself to acknowledge it, however. Sullenly he set down the apples and peanuts, murmuring, "I never did it before, anyhow!"

"No, nor never will again, I'm sure, child! This'll be a lifelong lesson to ye," returned the old woman as she put the dimes back into his hand. "Go right home with them now, an' tell yer mother all about it."

"Tell my mother!" faltered Tom, doubtful of the consequences of such a confession.

"Yes. She'll be gentle with ye, never fear, if ye are really sorry."

"Indeed I am, Mrs. Barry," declared Tom, quite breaking down at last.

"I'm certain ye are, child!" continued the good woman, heartily. "An' when ye get home, go to yer own little room, an' there on yer bended knees ask God to forgive ye. Make up yer mind to shun bad company for the future; an' never, from this hour, will we speak another word about this—save ye may come an' say: 'I've done as ye bid me, Mrs. Barry. It's all hunkey dory!'"

The old woman smiled with grim humor as she found herself quoting the boy's favorite slang expression.

Tom laughed in spite of himself, so funny did it sound from her lips; but at the same time he drew his jacket sleeve across his eyes, which had grown strangely dim, and said: "I will, Mrs. Barry. You may trust me: I will."

And Tom did. From that day he and the honest old applewoman were better friends than ever. Meanwhile her trade improved so much that before long she was able to set up a genuine stand, with an awning to replace the faithful umbrella. Here she carried on a thriving business for several years. Tom, though now a student at St. Jerome's College, often bought apples and peanuts from her.

"You see that old woman?" said he to a friend one day. "Doesn't look much like an angel, does she? And yet," continued Tom, earnestly, "she proved a second Guardian Angel to me once, and I'll bless her all my life for it."

The Evil Advisor

Scene I

Thomas. What's your hurry, Frank? Stop a minute.

Frank. I can't stay! Father sent me with this letter to the railroad depot.

Thomas. Well, the depot won't run away.

Frank. But the cars will; there's a gentleman going to New York who promised to carry this letter, and there's money in it for my brother.

Thomas. But don't you see it's but ten minutes past three; the cars don't start till four, and you have time enough for what I want of you.

Frank. Well, what do you want?

Thomas. Just step in here to see the wild beasts with me. You have not seen them, have you?

Frank. No; I'll go when I come back from my errand.

Thomas. No, you can't; for then it will be time for me to take my writing lesson.

Frank. Then I'll go with you tomorrow.

Thomas. No you can't, for this is the last day of the exhibition.

Frank. Is it? That's too bad! I did not know there were any beasts in town till today. How many are there?

Thomas. Ever so many; there's a polar bear, and an elephant, and a most beautiful rhinoceros—

Frank. I have seen a rhinoceros, and he is the ugliest creature that ever was; his skin sits as loosely upon him as a sailor's trousers.

Thomas. Well, there's a royal tiger—

Frank. Is there? I never saw a royal tiger.

Thomas. Oh, he's a beauty!—all yellow and covered with black stripes. Then there are little leopards, playing just like kittens; and—there! do you hear that? That's the lion roaring!

Frank. What a loud noise he makes! How long will it take to see them all?

Thomas. Oh, not half an hour; and it won't take you five minutes to go down to the depot afterwards, if you run as fast as you can.

Frank. Are there any monkeys?

Thomas. Plenty of them! the funniest monkeys you ever saw; they make all sorts of faces.

Frank. Well—I don't know—what if I should be too late for the cars?

Thomas. No danger of that, I tell you; the clock up there is too fast, it's all out of order; and, besides, you might see half the beasts while you are standing here thinking about it looking up the street and down the street.

Frank. Well, come along, then. Where's your money?

Thomas. Oh, I don't pay! I got acquainted with the door keeper after I had been in twice, and now he lets me in for nothing every time I bring a fellow that does pay.

Frank. Oho! Well, I suppose it's a quarter of a dollar, and I have one somewhere in my pockets. (Pulling out his handkerchief to search for the money, he drops the letter.) Ah, here it is! Come, Tom; no time to be lost. Mind you do not let me stay too long.

They go into the menagerie. Frank's father, passing along, picks up the letter, examines it, looks round for Frank, and passes hastily away.

Scene II

After some time the boys come out.

Thomas. You did not see half of them, you were in such a hurry and worry.

Frank. I know it. Are you sure that clock is too fast, Tom?

Thomas. I don't know—I suppose so—the clocks are wrong half the time.

Frank. Why, you told me it was too fast, Tom! and now I'm very sure that I shall be too late. I wish I hadn't gone in.

Thomas. Well, why don't you move, then? What are you rummaging after?

Frank. Why, after my letter. I'm sure I put it in this pocket. What in the name of wonder has become of it?

Thomas. Look in the other pocket.

Frank. It isn't there; nor in my hat. What shall I do?

Thomas. Why, you can't have lost it, can you?

Frank. I have lost it; I am as sure as can be I had it in this very pocket just before I met you and now it's gone.

Thomas. Perhaps somebody stole it in the crowd.

Frank. That's comfort! There was ever so much money in it, for I heard father talking about it at dinner-time.

Thomas. Oh, I'll tell you what's become of it.

Frank. What? what?

Thomas. Why, I guess the elephant took it out of your pocket.

Frank. You ought to be ashamed to stand there laughing, after you have got me into such a scrape! I have a great mind to go in again and look all round.

Thomas. They won't let you in again unless you pay.

Frank. O Tom! what will my father say to me? Where shall I look? I wish I had never heard of the beasts. There was no comfort in looking at them, for I was thinking of the cars all the time; and now my letter is lost, and brother Henry's money, and all; and what will father do to me?

Thomas. What's the use of telling him anything about it? He'll never know whether the letter went or not, if you don't say a word.

Frank. Yes, he will; my brother will write to inquire for the money.

Thomas. Well, and can't you say you gave the letter to the gentleman?

Frank. No, Tom; I can't do that. I can't tell a lie, and, above all, to my father.

Thomas. The more fool you! But you needn't look so sad about it. There's your father coming now. Run and tell him quick and get a whipping!

Frank. He will punish me, Tom; that he will. What shall I do?

Thomas. Take my advice. I'll tell a fib for you, and do you hold to it.

Frank. I never told a lie in my life, Tom.

Thomas. Then it's high time you did; you'll have to tell a great many before you die.

Frank. I don't believe that.

Thomas. Well, here's your father. Now see how I'll get you out of the scrape. That's right; keep staring up at the handbill on the wall.

Enter Father. Frank stares at the handbill.

Father. Why, Frank, you have run yourself out of breath. I trust that letter will go safely, for your brother wants the money very much.

Thomas. Frank was just in time, sir. The cars were just starting.

Father. Oh, you went with him, did you?

Thomas. Yes, sir; and I saw the gentleman put the

Rare Catholic Stories

letter in his pocket-book very carefully. I fancy it will go safe enough.

Father. I fancy it will. What is in that handbill, Frank, that interests you so much?

Frank. I don't know, sir.

Father. What's the matter, my boy?

Frank. I can't stand it, Father! I can't stand it! I had rather take ten whippings, Tom, any day, than— than—

Father. Ho, ho! What is all this?

Thomas. You are a fool, Frank.

Frank. I know I am a fool; but I can't tell a lie. I lost the letter, Father. I went to see the wild beasts with Tom, and lost the letter.

Father. And this precious fellow wanted you to deceive me about it, did he? Frank, I would willingly lose a dozen letters, with ten times as much money in them, for the pleasure of finding you resist this temptation! Come here, my boy, and leave off crying. I found the letter, and carried it myself to the depot in time for the cars. I can forgive your folly, since it has not ended in a base lie, but remember one thing: I shall not forgive you if, hereafter, you associate with this bad boy!

(To Thomas.) Begone, sir! I am glad to see shame on your face. Had my boy taken your advice, he, too, would have been at this moment a liar; but he can still hold up his head, and his heart is light in his bosom.

Tilderee

Part I

Quite happy indeed was the home of Tilderee Prentiss, though it was only a rough log house on a ranch, away out in Indian Territory. Her father was employed by the owner of the ranch. Her mother's duties included the management of a small dairy and poultry yard, the products of which were sold at the military post.

There were two other children: Peter, thirteen years old; and Joan, who had just passed her eleventh birthday. They took care of the fowl, and were proud when at the end of the week they could bring to their mother a large basket of eggs to carry to the Fort.

As the youngest in the family, six-year-old Tilderee had no chores, although the family thought she did a good deal—that is, all except Joan. For Tilderee seemed to make everybody else's burden lighter by her merriness, her funny sayings, and loving little ways. Yet she was continually getting into mischief; and to see her running to and fro, eager to be of use, but always lending a little hindering hand to everything, one would hardly consider her a help.

How frequently Mrs. Prentiss laughed, though

with tears in her eyes, as she thought of the time when Tilderee, a toddling baby, was nearly drowned by tumbling head-foremost into a pailful of foaming milk! How frightened Papa was at the discovery that his mischievous daughter had been at his ammunition chest and played dolls with the cartridges!

Peter and Joan could add their stories, too. Peter would tell how vexed he had been when she let his mustang out of the enclosure, "because," she said, "Twinkling Hoofs needs a scamper as well as anybody; and he was trying to open the gate with his nose." Joan would tell how she dallied in the morning playing hide-and-seek, refusing to have her face washed and her tangled hair brushed into shining curls; this, too, when Joan was in the greatest hurry to go and give the fluffy chicks and the grave old fowl their breakfast.

It was very well for Peter to say, "What should we do without Tilderee?" If she bothered him he could take his rifle and go shooting with Abe, the old scout; or jump upon Twinkling Hoofs and gallop all over the ranch. How would he like the midget to tag after him all day, to have the care of her when mother went to the Fort to sell the butter and eggs? "Indeed *I* could get on very well without the little plague," Joan sometimes grumbled—"just for a *teenty* bit of a while," she added hastily; for she really loved her little sister dearly. Joan tried hard to be patient, but she had a quick temper, and occasionally forgot her good resolutions. This happened one day when her mother had gone to dispose of the dairy products.

Joan had a lovely French doll. Mrs. Miller, the wife of one of the officers at the Fort brought it to her from Chicago; and the little girl regarded it as more precious than all the family possessions combined. What, then, was her consternation this morning to see Fudge dangling the fair Angelina by the blue silk dress, which he held between his teeth, and Tilderee following in wild pursuit! Joan rushed out and rescued her treasure; but, alas! the doll was beyond repair. She picked up a stick and started after the dog, but Tilderee interfered.

"Oh, please, dear Joan!" she cried. "Fudge isn't the most to blame. I took Angelina. I s'pose he pulled off the wig and broke the arm, but I pushed the eyes in; didn't mean to, though—was only trying to make them open and shut. Tilderee's so sorry, Joan!"

The explanation ended with a contrite sob. But the sight of the child's tears only irritated Joan the more. She said excitedly: "Tilderee Prentiss, you're a naughty, naughty girl! I wish you didn't live here. I wish mother had let you go with the lady at the Fort who wanted to adopt you. I wish I hadn't any little sister at all!"

Tilderee stopped crying, and stood gazing at the angry girl in astonishment; then, swallowing a queer lump that came in her throat, and with a sorrowful look on her face, she lisped slowly: "Very well. P'rhaps some day Tilderee'll go away and never come back again!"

She turned and went into the house, with Fudge at her heels.

Joan remained disconsolately weeping over the ill-fated Angelina. But, somehow, she did not feel any better for having yielded to her anger. "Tilderee deserved a good scolding," she said to herself over and over again. Still there was a weight upon her heart, for her conscience reproached her for those unkind, bitter words. After a while, remembering that she had been cautioned not to let Tilderee out of her sight, she started to look for her. The culprit was discovered in a corner of the kitchen, lecturing Fudge for running away with Angelina.

"Never meddle with what does not belong to you!" she said, shaking her forefinger and giving him an occasional tap on the nose. He listened dutifully, as if he were the sole transgressor.

Ashamed of having allowed her indignation to carry her so far, Joan, with an effort, managed to say, as if nothing had happened: "Come, Tilderee! Watch at the window for father, while I get dinner ready."

Tilderee at once sprang to her feet cheerily, threw her arms around Joan's waist, and held up her cheek for the kiss of forgiveness.

As soon as her mother returned, Tilderee related the morning's occurrence herself. "Fudge and me broke Joan's beauty doll. We didn't mean to, and we're awful sorry—honest and true we are!"

"But that will not mend Angelina," said Mrs. Prentiss, gravely.

Tilderee hung her head. She now realized for the first time that, no matter how grieved we are, we can not always repair the wrong we have done. Mrs. Prentiss now talked very seriously to her little daughter, and Tilderee promised to be less meddlesome and more obedient in the future.

"Fudge and me wants to be good," she said, penitently; "but we forgets. P'rhaps if our names were something else 'sides Tilderee and Fudge, we might be better."

"I'm afraid Fudge is a hard case," sighed her mother, restraining a smile; "but I expect we ought to call you Matilda as you were christened. You can pray to your name saint to help you."

The little lass was delighted, and from that time strove to insist upon her proper title. But it was not easy to drop the pet name, and Tilderee she was oftenest called. For several days she tried very hard to be good; she said her prayers with special earnestness, always closing with: "Please, God, take care of Tilderee, and keep her and Fudge out of mischief."

Joan, on her part, endeavored to be more gentle with her little sister; for she could not think of the incident without feeling uncomfortable about the way she had spoken to Tilderee.

The two girls were not allowed to go beyond the enclosure which surrounded the house, unless accompanied by their father or mother. The few Indians in the vicinity had hitherto been peaceable and friendly; but it was considered well to be cautious. When Mrs. Prentiss, mounted on the old grey horse, rode to the Fort to sell her butter and eggs, Peter went with her on Twinkling Hoofs; and each took the precaution to carry a pistol for self-defence in case of attack.

This being the state of affairs, great was the alarm when it became evident that Tilderee was missing. The ranch was a scene of intense excitement when, after an exploration of the neighborhood, the child was not found. The news spread like a prairie fire. The settlers for miles around joined the party which set out to continue the search. The poor mother was frantic, and Joan cried as though her heart would break.

Fudge had disappeared also. Had he gone with Tilderee? There was a grain of comfort in the suggestion; yet, even so, what could a poor baby do, astray and with no other defender? Evening came, and still there was no trace of the child. All through the night they continued to seek her, guided by the light of the stars and the glimmer of their pine torches. But in vain.

Part II

On that memorable day, shortly after the mid-day meal, if mother had not been so absorbed by the discovery that wee, blundering fingers had sprinkled sugar instead of salt over her new batch of butter— if she had glanced out of the doorway, she would have seen a figure tripping down the trail in happy unconcern, with Fudge gambolling along in front.

Tilderee had no intention of running away; but it was so easy to forget that she had passed the bounds which love had set for her, when the May breezes seemed to beset her to frolic with them, and from the midst of a patch of yellow wild flowers arose a flight of golden butterflies. What fun to chase them! Fudge thought so too, and a merry pursuit followed. Tired and out of breath, Tilderee paused at last. They were now half a mile from home, but neither turned to look back.

"Fudge, I'm going to pick a lovely bouquet for mother," Tilderee confided to him. He sniffed his approval, and trotted after her as she collected the bright blossoms. Now she left the prairie, and climbed Sunset Hill in search of prettier posies. Beyond this rocky knoll was an oak wood, from the direction of which came the noise of running water. At the sound Tilderee remembered that she was thirsty. "Come, Fudge," she said, "let us go and find the brook." The little girl pushed on, and soon came to a small stream.

After a refreshing drink, Tilderee chose a seat upon a log and rested. All at once the child became aware that the woods had grown darker; the sunlight no longer glanced in among the green boughs. Next she realized that it must be a great while since she'd eaten. With the sense of hunger came a feeling of dismay. Where was she, and how should she get home? "It must be most supper time, Fudge," she said, choking down a sob. The little dog thrust his cold nose into her hand, as if to say encouragingly: "Trust me, and I will lead you back." He began to sniff the ground; and, having found the scent, endeavored to prevail upon his young mistress to follow his guidance. But Tilderee was sure that she knew best. "No, Fudge," she called; "not that way. This is the right path, I'm sure. Come quick!"

They wandered on; at every step the surroundings grew wilder, the way more rocky and precipitous. In her baby innocence, Tilderee knew nothing of the perils of Indians, wild cattle, and countless dangers. She only felt that she was weary and chilled, and faint for want of food. "Oh Fudge, if we could only get home to mother!" she moaned. "Tilderee's so tired and sleepy, and it will be dark night soon."

Dispirited, Tilderee dragged herself to a nook under a projecting rock, which seemed to promise a slight shelter from the cold night air. "I 'xpect it's time for night prayers," she said, with a tremor in her voice. She knelt upon the damp ground, made the Sign of the Cross, and, clasping her hands, repeated the "Our Father" and "Hail Mary" more devoutly than ever before. When she came to the special little petition at the close, "Please, God, take care of Tilderee, and keep her and Fudge out of mischief," she broke down, and, weeping convulsively, threw her arms around the neck of her loyal playmate, exclaiming, "Oh Fudge! if we ever get safe home we'll never be naughty again, will we?"

Drawing the plaid shawl from her shoulders, she spread it over herself like a blanket; sparing a corner for Fudge, however, who stationed himself upon it, prepared to ward off all dangers from his charge. And thus she fell asleep in that lonely wilderness.

* * * *

During the long night, while the searching party was scouring the country, Mrs. Prentiss remained at home, keeping a fire on the kitchen hearth, and everything ready to gladden and revive her darling in case the dear little rover should find her way back of her own accord. How many times she started up, thinking she heard the patter of childish feet! But Joan would murmur sadly: "It is only the wind or the call of a bird." At which the unhappy woman would sigh: "Let us say the Rosary again." Joan, whose face was stained with tears, and her eyes swollen and red from weeping, responded as best she could between her sobs.

Poor Joan! Amid all her thoughts that night, one scene was ever before her: the picture of herself, as she snatched up the doll and spoke harshly: "You naughty girl! I wish you didn't live here! I wish I hadn't any little sister at all!" Well, her wish had come true: Tilderee was gone. There was no "little plague" to vex or bother Joan tonight. Angelina!— She never wanted even to see the doll again. Tilderee might get up a "make-believe" funeral for the doll if she came back,—ah, *if!* And then Joan would put her head down upon the table or a chair, whichever happened to be near, or hide her face in the folds of her apron, and cry: "What shall I do without Tilderee! Oh, if God will only give her back to us, I will never say a cross or angry word again!"

Dawn brought no news of the lost child, and the dreary night of suspense was succeeded by a day of anguish. The seekers at length despaired of gaining trace or tidings of her, and agreed that it was useless to continue the search.

"She must have fallen over a precipice," said one of the men.

"If so, we should have met with some sign—" argued another, hesitating at the thought of what that sign might be.

"It is probable that she has been stolen by the Indians," said Lieutenant Miller; "and we must adopt other means to recover her."

Once more dusk was approaching, and they were about to turn back, when—hark! there was a shout from the borders of the canyon beyond. A few moments before, Abe, the old scout, had disappeared in that direction. As he pressed onward he presently discovered that, in a wavering line, the brambles seemed to have been recently trodden down. A little farther on, almost hidden among the briers and dry leaves, lay a withered wild flower, like those that grew in the plain below; and farther still, caught upon a bush, was a bit of the fringe of a shawl. As he stood still, he heard a sound amid the brush; it was a little dog crawling down toward a spring of water in a hollow.

"Fudge!" he called, softly. The dog started, and, with many backward glances to make sure that he was following, led the way to a high rock which formed a sort of canopy above the bank. There he found the lost child. At first he feared she might be dead, so still she lay; but when he whispered gently, "Tilderee!" the eyelids opened; the dull eyes lit up in recognition, and she smiled a weak little smile.

Abe's cheery voice rang out, calling, "Found! found!" and the woods and cliffs made merry with the echoes. His companions hastened toward the ravine; but he met them half way, carrying the little one in his arms.

What a shout of joy greeted the sight! What thankfulness filled the heart of Mr. Prentiss as he held Tilderee in his arms! Peter lept upon Twinkling Hoofs and sped away like the wind, "to tell them at home." Who could describe the emotions of the fond mother when, half an hour later, she clasped her darling to her breast? What a happy stillness reigned in the house for hours, while Tilderee was tenderly brought back from the verge of starvation!

As for Joan, it seemed to her that there could never be any mourning or sadness again. When she had done everything possible for Tilderee, she lavished attentions upon Fudge, and announced to him that henceforth he was to be called Fido (faithful); at which he wagged his tail, as if he found the role of hero quite to his liking. Joan's heart was so light that she wished everyone in the world could share her happiness; but whether she laughed or chattered, or hummed a little song to herself, the refrain of all this gladness was "Oh, how good God is! How good God is!"

George White's Ten Dollars

George White had been saving his spending money for a long time; in fact, ever since his uncle had given him a beautiful little iron safe, made just like those in his father's office.

One morning he opened his treasure, and on counting it over, he found he had the large sum of ten dollars. "Now," he said, "I can buy anything I want! I must speak to Papa about it."

It was winter, and the ground was covered with ice and snow, so that whenever George went out of doors his mother was careful to see him well wrapped up. He loved to stay out in the open air rather than in the warm house, as his rosy cheeks and bright eyes plainly showed.

He was very fond of skating and coasting, but he had lost one of his skates and his sled was broken. So that evening, as they sat around the tea-table, he said: "Papa, may I spend my ten dollars for a new sled and a pair of skates?"

His father replied, "The money is yours, my son; you may spend it as you please; but tomorrow morning I am going some distance in the city, and intended taking you."

"O Papa, I should like that!"

"Then you must not buy your sled and skates until our return."

George willingly consented; but he could not understand why his father should wish him to wait until they returned, when he could so easily make his purchases on the way.

The next day George prepared to accompany his father; and while his mother handed him his overcoat and fur cap, and wrapped a warm comforter around his neck, he was thinking of the fun he would have with his new sled.

"When I am coasting," he said to himself, "I will lend my skates to Andrew O'Connor, and when I am skating, I will lend him my sled." Now Andrew O'Connor was much poorer than George White, and his widowed mother could hardly afford to buy him toys so expensive. George's resolution, therefore, proved he had a kind heart.

By this time his father was ready for the walk, and taking George's hand, they waved a smiling good-bye. George and his father walked on, passing the splendid houses of the rich, and the large stores wherein are to be found all things rare and costly for those who have money to buy them. Presently they reached a large toy store, where, suspended in the window, was a handsome sled.

Snow-bird, the name of the sled, was on the seat, and the sled itself was painted red and white. "O Papa!" said George, "here is just what I want. Let us go in and get it."

"Wait, my son," said Mr. White, "until we come back."

They walked a little further, and then leaving the bright, gay avenue, turned into a narrow, crooked street, on either side of which were small, dirty, and

Rare Catholic Stories

miserable dwellings, with here and there a tall tenement. Before one of the small houses, Mr. White paused, made a few inquiries, and entered.

George, still holding his father's hand, went slowly up the broken staircase. On the upper floor, they turned, and knocked at a door near the end of the hall. A faint voice from within said, "Come in," and they stepped into the room. The sight that met their gaze would have moved a harder heart than Little George's.

In one corner, on a bed of straw, lay a man feeble and wasted with sickness. Four little half-clothed children, with wan, sickly faces, were trying to play in another corner of the room, and weeping by the sick man's bed sat a pale and slender woman.

George's father spoke to her, and from her lips heard a sad tale of poverty and distress. A friend of his, belonging to the worthy "Conference of St. Vincent de Paul," whose object is to visit the sick in their homes, had already told Mr. White of this suffering family, and he had come to relieve their misery and to see for himself what were their most urgent needs.

He determined to send a doctor at once. George stole up to his father's side and whispered, "O Papa! give them my ten dollars!" When they left the house, Mr. White said, "Are you willing to give up your sled and skates for the whole winter, and spend the money for this poor family?"

"Yes," said George, "I am not only willing, but I want to do it with all my heart."

"Very well, then, my son, you shall buy meat, and bread, and milk, and clothing for the children, and I will take care of their parents."

In the poor room that night were light, and fire, and food, and on the pale mother's face, a happy smile. And George was happier after having done this good deed than if he had bought the handsomest sled and skates in the world.

Happy·Go·Lucky

Part I

"Well, that beats all I ever heard tell of! A young lady, you say—one of them that looks just as fresh and fine as a bunch of posies? Don't yer think she's a little onsettled in her mind, Dave?"

"Why? Because Miss Evans has rigged up the big, front room in the basement of her father's house; made a jolly parlor of it, and invited all of us ragged chaps to spend the evenin' with her? Not a speck, Lucky," concluded Dave, with a chuckle.

"Sorry I can't go, but my dress suit isn't quite up to the mark, yer see," explained Lucky, glancing at his tattered jacket and trousers.

"Oh, yer'd better come! The room is splendid and warm, has lots of light, and plenty of chairs and small tables. The furniture is not done up in satin; good hard pine, that's all. And games, and papers, and jingo, yer'll hardly believe it—but a *bony-fidy* piano! Miss Evans laughs at it, and says it's pretty well used up. But the fellers get as much fun out of it as if it was a whole brass band."

"H'm! 'praps I will look in sometime," replied his friend, who had an ear for music.

"There's hot cocoa and sandwiches," added Dave, briefly.

Lucky's mouth began to water. "Let's start now!" he suggested.

"Oh-ho! yer can't. 'Tisn't the night. It's only three times a week," answered Dave. "I say, Lucky," he called with some embarrassment, "yer'll have to fix up some, though. They're kinder stylish, yer know. Clean hands and face—that's the rule."

"Pshaw! too much bother!" replied Lucky, in a discouraged tone.

"Tain't so hard, after yer're used to it; and we've got to put up with somethin'," said Dave, anxious that his comrade should not throw aside the benefits offered to him, even for this grave objection.

"Well, I'll see," consented Lucky; and he turned and ran down the dark alley, in the depths of which was his home.

The next evening the two boys made their way to the hospitable house of Miss Annie Evans. They were wonderfully "spruced up," as Dave expressed it, casting an approving glance at Lucky. The latter caught the look, and his face glowed with satisfaction.

"What a pair of begrimed little fellows!" thought the young lady who received them. Miss Evans' manner did not betray her impression. She only nodded and smiled at Dave.

"I've brought a friend, ma'am," said he.

"I'm glad you did, Dave," she answered, cordially.

Lucky thought he had never heard so glad and cheery a voice.

"Come and sit here," said she, giving the newcomer a place beside her. "And what is your name?" she asked, looking at him steadily with a pair of bright, kind, brown eyes.

"Happy-go-Lucky."

"Well, that *is* an odd name," she declared, laughing. "Haven't you any other?"

"Yes," he admitted, as if trying to recollect something entirely unfamiliar. "Guess it's Ben," he ventured at last, "Ben Saunders."

"Where are your father and mother?"

"Dead," he mumbled, stoically.

"Where do you live?"

"In Lanigan's attic."

Annie sighed. It seemed useless to attempt to obtain any further information.

"Why do they call you Happy-go-Lucky?" she continued.

"Because—because—" he faltered, then grew crimson, and gazed shamefacedly at the gaping toes of his worn-out shoes.

"Never mind. I suppose it is because you are always fortunate, is it not?" said Miss Evans, dismissing the subject.

Lucky assented.

The evening passed only too quickly. To Lucky it was the most pleasant he had ever spent. There were about twenty boys present. Many of them played games at the little tables, others thrummed on the piano, or sang the popular songs of the day. The cocoa and sandwiches were an important feature of the entertainment, to which the guests did full justice.

The noise and confusion rendered the place a very bedlam. Amid the din, the young lady moved about serenely, chatting now with one little fellow, now with another.

Annie Evans was baptized a Catholic, but her father, a widower, and an easy-going, good-natured man, did not belong to any church, and his wife had died suddenly, without an opportunity to provide for the education of the child in her own faith.

Annie liked society. She was petted, admired, and spoiled by the fashionable circle in which she moved. Yet she was not contented. She wanted, she declared, "an object in life." At this, friends shrugged their shoulders; but Mr. Evans, who idolized his daughter, said: "If you must have a hobby, Annie, go ahead; I reckon I can afford it."

"Then, papa," admitted the girl, "I want—Oh! I want to fit up the unused room downstairs, and have the street gamins here in the evenings. They have no friends. I want to help them—to do them good."

Mr. Evans gave a prolonged whistle of astonishment. "Go on, my dear," he consented at last, seeing how important it was to her. So "Annie's receptions to ragamuffins," as her father playfully called them, began.

"I tell yer, Dave, guess Miss Evans don't 'xactly know what kind o' fellers we are," said Lucky that night, as they went out into the darkness.

"No," replied Dave, indifferently. "I 'xpect she thinks we're of the 'poor but honest' sort."

"By Jove, but didn't I feel cheap when she asked me why I was called Happy-go-Lucky!" volunteered his companion, confidentially.

Dave burst into a loud guffaw. "Wouldn't she open those pretty eyes o' hers," he cried, "if she knew it was because yer always have such grand good luck in

filchin' small things from Tom, Dick, and Harry—
that it makes no odds how bad a scrape yer get into,
yer manage to wriggle out o' the way o' the cop!"

Lucky was surprised to find himself uneasy about
the matter. "It won't do," he said, at length. "We can't
go there if we keep on this way. We'll have to take
up another profession."

"What, I'd like to know?" asked Dave, incredulously.

"Oh, selling papers, or blacking boots, or somethin'," answered Lucky, with decision.

"There's plenty o' time to think about that," returned Dave, lazily. "Like as not Miss Evans'll drop
the whole thing before long. Such people always do.
Better see if it's goin' to last before yer get so awful
pertic'lar 'bout not cheatin' her."

Lucky made no reply to this scrap of worldly
wisdom, and the two trudged along in silence.

Miss Evans assuredly was ignorant of many
things about her boys. They joked among themselves
at her simplicity. By degrees, however, she learned in
a general way, and once or twice from personal experience, that her questionable *protégés* were given
to pilfering; to all the petty vices; some even were in
danger of becoming hardened little criminals.

Lucky soon became Miss Evans' favorite, though
she treated him in all things as she did the others.
When his face was clean—which happened rarely—
he was a handsome boy, with an angelic expression;
but he speedily revealed himself the most audacious
little rascal of them all. None tried her patience, nor
saddened her, so often. After she had caught him in
various peccadilloes, and rescued him several times

from the police court, she was inclined to give him up as a hopeless case.

And yet, she felt there was some good in the boy. Sometimes when she took him to task he would say, contritely: "Indeed I'll try to be better. Yer see, Miss Annie, if I had any one to talk to me as yer do, I'd never have got so bad." Once, when she chanced to glance at his grimy little hand, which she had taken in her soft white one, she said reproachfully: "So small, yet so black, Lucky!" Whereupon, he hid it behind his back; showing that he had taken a deeper meaning from the speech than she intended. On another occasion, when she concluded an appeal with, "God loves you, Lucky, and wants you to be good," turning to look at him, she saw an expression of intense astonishment upon his face, as if the words were a revelation.

Part II

As their kind friend persevered in the work she had undertaken, Dave and Lucky felt it was time to go into the boot-blacking business—or rather, Miss Evans went into it, and took the two boys as partners; she was the moneyed member of the firm.

Her two especial *protégés* seemed at last to be really trying to improve. Suddenly, Lucky disappeared. Annie had become accustomed to periodical "breaks for liberty," so she now forbore to ask for the truant; but she was anxious and distressed. A week passed; still there was no sign of him; at last she asked Dave for news.

"I dunno," he replied. "Haven't seen him myself for some time. Gone off on a vacation, I guess."

She waited several days longer. Then she said: "Dave, I want you to hunt up Ben for me. Something may have happened to him."

The following day, Dave plucked her by the sleeve, saying: "I've found him, ma'am. He's sick. He went to old Missus Fay, the washerwoman, and she took him in."

Annie immediately sought her father, and begged to be allowed to go see Lucky without delay. Her father consented, but insisted that she take the housekeeper, Hester, with her.

After much traversing of dirty streets and crooked alleys, they came to the dilapidated house to which Dave had directed them. "Missus Fay has gone out to work," the neighbors informed them.

Mounting the rickety stairs to the attic, the visitors came to a dimly lit corner under the eaves. Here upon a wretched bed lay Lucky, burning with fever, and talking incoherently. His eyes, unnaturally bright and roving, stared at Annie wildly at first; but presently, a smile of recognition made the flushed face radiant. It was only for a moment. The look of delight faded; he began to wander again.

Gently, Annie strove to soothe him, to cool the poor little aching head, and bring rest to the weary, childish frame. After a time, as she chanced to raise him, to smooth his pillow, she caught sight of a tiny object hung about his neck. With some curiosity, she stooped to examine what seemed a tarnished bit of silver. It was a medal, like one she had long ago seen her old nurse wear.

"Hester," she said, "the child must be a Catholic! He is dangerously ill. You will have to go for a priest."

With some misgivings, the elderly housekeeper finally started out, without knowing where to go. By dint of many inquiries she found the rectory of St. Joseph's Church, and soon returned with Father Neville.

The good priest uttered an exclamation of pity and surprise, as he beheld the fever-stricken figure of the child, and the beautiful girl bending over him. There was something familiar, too, about Lucky, and in a minute he recollected to have seen him before.

"I thought from this medal, sir, that the boy might be a Catholic," said Annie softly.

Father Neville observed him closely. "No," returned he, "I do not think so. Yet how strangely things come to pass! I gave the little fellow that medal a year or more ago. He came for me one night, in the height of a winter's storm, to ask me to visit an old man who was dying, and whom he had taken care of with remarkable devotedness. I hoped to keep track of him, but he vanished, as it were, and I was never able to discover a trace of him."

Annie appeared impressed by the coincidence. "He is very ill, is he not?" she questioned.

"In the last stages of typhoid-pneumonia, I should say," replied the priest and, after regarding her gravely, added: "I doubt if he will live more than an hour or two."

"What can be done for him?" she asked, addressing Father Neville.

"You did well to send for me," he answered. "Listen!"

Lucky had begun to talk again, in a rambling, fitful way, yet showing that some thought was uppermost in his mind and struggling for expression.

"No, Miss Annie," he raved; "Happy-go-Lucky— never did nothin' good—always wicked! Just look at those hands!" he cried, starting up, and stretching out his hot little palms. "Yer said so, and it's true, sure. 'So small and so black!' Too bad, too bad! Very sorry. Wish I could begin again! I'd try to keep 'em clean, yer bet!"

At this, the small clenched fist beat against the wall with determined reiteration, till Annie caught and held it, to spare the child the pain he was inflicting on himself. The act made him gaze blankly at her.

"Do yer think they'll let me in up yonder?" he asked earnestly. "Miss Annie's rules was that a feller's hands must be washed. But—I 'xpect they're more patic'lar yonder. Wonder if it's as bright and pleasant as at Miss Annie's? Why, yes," he continued; "Of course—it must be. Wish I'd been taught what it was like! Miss Annie said, 'God loves you, Lucky.' Queer, aint it? Wish I'd known it afore!"

For a brief space he lay silent. He was visibly growing weaker. By and by he recommenced, in a fainter voice:

"When I help Missus Fay with the big basket of clothes she carries home—poor old woman, she's not fit to drag 'em along herself,—she allus says, 'Heaven bless ye, me b'y!' Curious! And Tim. My, but it's long sence I thought of old Tim! Jimini, what a time I had takin' care of him! Couldn't let a poor feller die alone, though. Goodness, but wasn't he cross! The rheumatiz is mighty hard on tempers, yer know," concluded he, with a sagacious nod at Annie.

"And," he went on, growing intensely serious, "there was the night I went for the priest! Thought I'd never get there, it stormed so. But Tim was dyin'—and I wasn't goin' to let him ask for a thing twice. Came back with Father—forget his name. Mighty nice man, though. After that, a change came over Tim—got kinder mild and satisfied like. Ah! That night he was gone. And his last words was, 'God reward ye, Ben—God reward ye!' Do yer think He will?" inquired the little fellow, abruptly, fixing a piercing glance upon Father Neville.

"Assuredly, my boy," rejoined the priest, gently.

"Why!" exclaimed the dying child, "Yer're the very priest what gave me the medal, and told me about the beautiful Lady! I used to try and make a picture of her in my mind."

"Ben," said Father Neville, "would you like to see her? Would you like her to take you to God? Shall I baptize you?"

"Will that make my hands white?" gasped the little fellow, eagerly.

"Yes! Hands, and heart, and soul, my child, no matter how blackened by wrong."

Lucky smiled a blissful assent. Scarce had the saving waters fallen upon his head, than he sank into a peaceful sleep, from which he never wakened here.

Annie watched until the end. At length, rising from her knees, she bent tenderly over the childish form; then, reverently taking the little medal, she allowed Hester to lead her away.

Annie was aroused to serious thought by the scene through which she had passed. She read and studied much, but a singular circumstance hastened her return to the Church. Several months had passed, when one night she had a strange dream. Lucky came to her, showed her his hands, now spotless and shining, and bade her delay no longer.

In after years, when asked what brought her back to the faith, Annie always answered, simply: "A little medal and Happy-go-Lucky."

Jack's Wood Pile

"Mother, I think I shall haul the wood down to the village tomorrow."

"Very well, my dear," answered his mother. "I shall have some chickens ready for you to take along."

Since the death of his father, Jack had been the chief support of his mother and his two little brothers. They lived at least four miles from the village, and not a neighbor was within a mile of them, and were it not for the whistle of the locomotive, as the trains passed through the cut below their house, the place would have been lonesome indeed.

Jack was very proud of his wood pile. It had cost him many weeks of hard work, for he had cut and sawed every stick of it himself, and upon it depended the winter's supply of food and clothing for the little family. "I have a cord more than Mother thinks there is," he whispered to his brothers "and with the money I get for that I mean to buy all sorts of nice things—apples and raisins—and maybe Mother will make us some mince-pies for Christmas."

The next day, Jack started with the first load of wood, his head full of plans for extra comforts for his mother and brothers. When he drew up in front of the little store in which the country folks traded their corn, wheat, and other produce for groceries and dry-goods, the owner was standing at the door.

"No, I do not want any wood," he said in answer to Jack's question. "I bought a piece of woodland last summer, and I have cut my own wood this year, and supplied everyone around here.—No, I do not want any chickens, either; but if you are very anxious to trade, I will take what you have at three cents a pound."

No wood wanted! Poor Jack could hardly keep back the tears; the scarf for his mother, the mittens for the boys, flannels, and other necessities were all gone in a minute. Three cents a pound for chickens! It would pay better to eat them than to sell them at that price. However, he parted with a few to get some things his mother could not well do without, and then turned his mules homeward.

Jack did not unload the wood when he reached home, but left it standing. Snow had been falling for some time, and as the boy walked toward the house, after putting his mules in the stable, the ground was quite white. In a few words, Jack told his mother of his failure to sell the wood, and then seated himself by the fire, resting his head on his hands.

"I do not know what we are going to do," he said after a while, in a tone that spoke more than his words.

"Nor I, Jack," said his mother, putting her arm tenderly round him; "but, my dear, we are not expected to know. It is only our Lord who knows. We must wait and trust."

"I wonder how things would go on if we would just sit down and trust."

"But we do not sit down and trust. We do our best, and when we have done that, all we can do is to trust. Those were almost the last words your dear father said to me. He saw what was coming, but he felt that God, who feeds the young ravens, would not forget us. Have faith and hope, Jack, my boy, have faith and hope."

The snow fell thick and fast through the night, and the following morning Jack could hardly make his way to the stable to feed the cow and the mules. When he did succeed in getting there, he met a sight that surprised him. In the railroad cut stood a long train of cars half-buried in the snow. A number of men were trying to clear a path before the engine, while, others were passing Jack's load of wood into the cars.

"Halloo!" cried a man who was directing the workmen, "do you know whose wood this is?"

"It is mine," replied Jack.

"Well, if you have any more, I want it,—all you have. Can you bring it here?"

"As soon as I can dig it out of the snow."

"My brakemen will help you," said the man, who was the conductor of the train. "We are in a bad fix. We have been here all night, and are likely to be here all day. My passengers must not freeze. Bring all the wood you can."

Jack hurried to give his mules their breakfast, and while they were eating, he ran to tell his mother the good news.

"Did I not tell you to have faith and hope?" said his mother. "Our dear Lord never forgets those who trust in Him."

Jack worked like a hero that morning, and when he carried the first armful of wood into a car, what a

shout of
welcome he
received from the
half-frozen passengers!

"See here," said the conduc-
tor, when the fires were well started, "do you know
where we can get something to eat?"

"We have plenty of chickens and potatoes and
cornmeal, and my mother can cook them," answered
Jack.

"And we will help, if she will let us," said three
ladies.

Jack's mother and the lady passengers were soon
at work, and before long steaming, mealy potatoes,
hot cornbread, and delicious fried chickens were
served to the grateful passengers.

About noon, the conductor bustled into the house.
"We are off soon," he said, "and I want to square ac-
counts with you. We pay three dollars and a half a
cord for wood. Just see what that amounts to. Then
there are three or four dozen chickens, bushels of

potatoes, and the best cornbread I ever tasted. I am in too great a hurry to figure it all out, but I guess this will pay for it," laying some bank-notes on the table. "If that is not right, just send to the address on this card. Good-bye! Thank you," and before Jack's mother could say a word the man hurried out.

When Jack ran down to see the train off, he was received with cheers.

"Here," said a man, picking up a train-boy's basket, "let us give them some books and papers—they are always welcome in the country."

"Yes, and so are other things," said a lady who had noticed the poverty of the house, "here is a shawl for Jack's mother."

That started it, and as the basket passed from one car to another, mittens, caps, scarfs, and overshoes were thrown in. Those who had nothing else to spare tied a little money in their handkerchiefs, and threw them in, and, last of all, one man gave an overcoat for Jack. Then the basket was lifted off the train, and put at the boy's feet, and with the passengers crying, "A merry Christmas, Jack!" and, "Three cheers for Jack's mother!" the train went on its way.